Skeeter Jones

A NOVEL by

Ronald "Butch" Vaughn

Smoking Duck Publications

DEDICATION

I would like to dedicate this book to the following people:

First, to my brother Jack. He was twelve years older than me. Jack was more than just a big brother. When I was young I thought the sun rose and set over his right shoulder. Later, we became friends. Later still, we became business partners. We didn't always agree on some of the smaller issues but when push came to shove, we both knew the other was always there. I will miss him immensely. Jack died in September 2020 at the age of eighty-nine.

To my friend for over thirty years, Joy McGay. She was one of the first people to encourage me to write my first book *BUTCH*. Joy always had a positive attitude, was upbeat, and had a smile on her face. Joy died in March 2020 at the age of ninety-one.

To my wife of fifty-nine years who gives me encouragement and a great deal of space to do my creative writing (as long as I help with the yard work). Thanks to her I have my book publishing team.

And most importantly, to Jesus Christ my Lord and Savior. He was crucified, died, rose from the grave, and sits at the right hand of God the Father. Read John 3:16 and Romans 3:23.

Also by Ronald “Butch” Vaughn

BUTCH, a memoir

Edited and Illustrated
by
Sherri Vaughn Petersmark

Do you have any idea how valuable an editor is to a writer? I really didn't. I read what other writers said about their editors but I didn't understand until I needed one.

I wrote the entire book beginning, middle, and end. All done. Then I brought Sherri in. She took one look and must have passed out. She corrected hundreds of misspelled words, grammar, and punctuation errors. It was a technical editor's nightmare. After the first edit, I thought we're done, right? No! She then had to do the content editing. She said, "You have to do more than tell a story, you have to bring the reader into the story. Give feeling to the characters, describe the setting." And much, much more.

Do you like the front and back covers? If so, thanks. I thought the idea of Skeeter coming toward you on the front and walking away was nice. Who drew Skeeter? Sherri (Vaughn) Petersmark. What a talent.

Hobo Codes

https://www.logodesignlove.com/hobo-signs-and-symbols

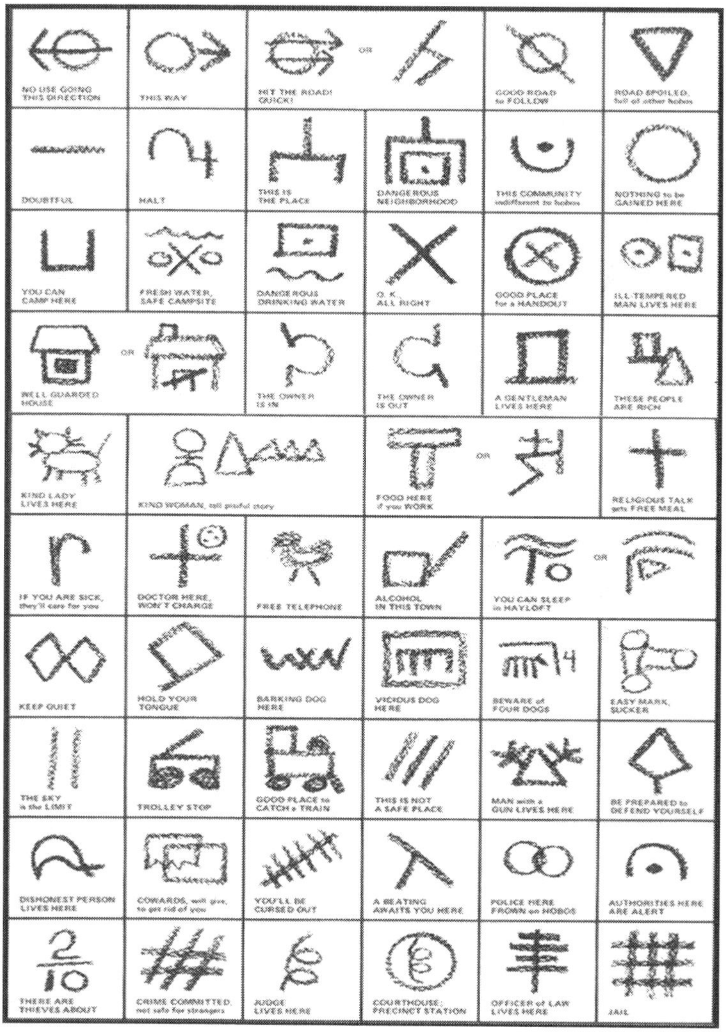

NO USE GOING THIS DIRECTION
THIS WAY
HIT THE ROAD! QUICK! OR
GOOD ROAD to FOLLOW
ROAD SPOILED, full of other hobos

DOUBTFUL
HALT
THIS IS THE PLACE
DANGEROUS NEIGHBORHOOD
THIS COMMUNITY indifferent to hobos
NOTHING to be GAINED HERE

YOU CAN CAMP HERE
FRESH WATER, SAFE CAMPSITE
DANGEROUS DRINKING WATER
O.K., ALL RIGHT
GOOD PLACE for a HANDOUT
ILL-TEMPERED MAN LIVES HERE

WELL GUARDED HOUSE OR
THE OWNER IS IN
THE OWNER IS OUT
A GENTLEMAN LIVES HERE
THESE PEOPLE ARE RICH

KIND LADY LIVES HERE
KIND WOMAN, tell pitiful story
FOOD HERE if you WORK OR
RELIGIOUS TALK gets FREE MEAL

IF YOU ARE SICK, they'll care for you
DOCTOR HERE, WON'T CHARGE
FREE TELEPHONE
ALCOHOL IN THIS TOWN
YOU CAN SLEEP in HAYLOFT OR

KEEP QUIET
HOLD YOUR TONGUE
BARKING DOG HERE
VICIOUS DOG HERE
BEWARE of FOUR DOGS
EASY MARK, SUCKER

THE SKY is the LIMIT
TROLLEY STOP
GOOD PLACE to CATCH a TRAIN
THIS IS NOT A SAFE PLACE
MAN with a GUN LIVES HERE
BE PREPARED to DEFEND YOURSELF

DISHONEST PERSON LIVES HERE
COWARDS, will give, to get rid of you
YOU'LL BE CURSED OUT
A BEATING AWAITS YOU HERE
POLICE HERE FROWN on HOBOS
AUTHORITIES HERE ARE ALERT

THERE ARE THIEVES ABOUT
CRIME COMMITTED, not safe for strangers
JUDGE LIVES HERE
COURTHOUSE; PRECINCT STATION
OFFICER of LAW LIVES HERE
JAIL

Skeeter Jones

Chapter 1

You wouldn't think that a person raised in a small mid-western town in the center of Michigan would murder someone, but he did. He killed three someones, as a matter of fact. He was a friend of mine. Skeeter Jones. His real name wasn't Skeeter, it was Grant, everyone just called him Skeeter, don't know why they just did. Let me tell you a little something about Skeeter and how I came to know him.

It was late spring of 1951. I was eleven years old at the time. My family, father Harold, mother Edna, brother Jack, and me, Ron, better known as Butch, lived in a very modest wood-frame house that my dad and grandfather built. It was located on the west side of Flint in a community known as Utley. Utley was composed mainly of lower-income, lower-educated families that migrated from the south to Flint, Michigan to work for General Motors. People used to refer to General Motors as Generous Motors because of the higher-paying jobs.

My father and brother started a small manufacturing business which my father ran part-time as well as worked full time at another job. The business had grown somewhat and Dad thought he needed to expand the business and get into a larger building. There was no room to expand the little two-car garage that housed the machine shop.

We were having dinner when out of the blue dad announced that we would be moving to the little town of Byron some twenty-five miles away. It might as well have been a million miles. Utley, a suburb of Flint and a rough and tumble community, to Byron, a village of five hundred, an easy-going laid-back farming community. It also meant I had to give up my relationship with Beverly, but that's a different story for a different time.

Byron was a sleepy little town where security and trust were abundant. Families didn't lock their houses or cars. Even the owner of the hardware would leave his store unlocked while he went home for lunch. If you needed something while he was out, you could simply go in, look around, find what you wanted, leave him a note telling him what you got, and pay for the item the next time you came into the store.

Byron was even a bit old-fashioned. When you shopped at the general store for groceries you would go to a counter and ask the storekeeper for the items you wanted and he would get them for you. There was a large jar of pickles on the counter, and a large block of cheese that was protected with a glass cover. If you wanted cheese the storekeeper would cut off the amount you wanted and wrap it in paper for you.

Byron was a great place to live and raise a family. A perfect place for a real Huckleberry Finn kid to live.

When we moved to Byron one of the first people I met was a guy by the name of Skeeter Jones. He was a happy-go-lucky skinny guy with light brown hair, almost never combed, and blue eyes.

Legend has it that Skeeter's house was the oldest structure in Byron. The legend goes on to state that there was an Indian attack on the village and it was destroyed except for the house on the hill. It was untouched. The owner of the house helped one of the Indians at one time and they didn't forget.

Shortly after I met Skeeter, his family moved four or five blocks away to a house located on the banks of the mighty Shiawassee River. The Shiawassee had several tributaries and one was the Byron Mill Pond that flowed through two dams. One was called the Little Dam and the other, yep, the Big Dam. Skeeter lived with his mother, father, three brothers, and four sisters. His father and two older brothers worked for the Grand Trunk Railroad in Durand seven miles north of Byron.

Skeeter living on the Shiawassee River was perfect for him. He loved to hunt, fish, and trap muskrats.

Not surprisingly, Skeeter and I went into the muskrat trapping business. We would set our traps on the banks of the Shiawassee River and Mill Pond. The Mill Pond happened to flow past the village cemetery.

Skeeter and I had about sixteen traps that we had to check twice a day, once in the early morning about sun up, and once in the evening about sundown. Trapping season was in the winter. It was cold, blowing snow type weather. We would take

turns checking the traps, or running the line as we called it. I would do the early run, Skeeter would do the late run, and the next day we would switch. We sold our muskrat hides to a local bait and fur buyer for the whopping price of seventy-five cents each.

Trapping muskrats wasn't much fun. We had to try and get to the traps before the muskrats could get loose. Once a muskrat was in the trap they would do anything to get out. It was a matter of life and death for them. They would chew off a foot to get free, leaving them with one less foot and Skeeter and me with one less muskrat.

When we got to a trap that had a muskrat, we had to get it out. You couldn't just reach down and take it out of the trap. It would be just a little angry about being trapped and would bite the living daylights out of you, so you had to hit it in the head with a club or shoot it with a twenty-two caliber rifle. Nasty business that muskrat trapping.

I finally decided to get out of the muskrat business. Remember we ran the line in the dark, in the winter, in the cemetery. All kinds of thoughts would go through your mind. The wind whistling, a branch falling. You knew someone was there to get you.

Skeeter and I were good friends for a couple of years. When I was about fourteen we sort of drifted apart. About that time Skeeter had enough of school. He was a pretty bright kid. He just didn't like school, so he quit. He went his way and I went mine. It seemed every few years our paths crossed.

After quitting school Skeeter got a job at a chicken farm not far from Byron where they processed chicken. Basically, that

meant they killed chickens, gutted them, cut them up, and sold them to stores. Not a very pleasant job.

After a few months of killing and gutting chickens, Skeeter decided a move was in order, so he joined the U.S. Army. Lucky for Skeeter, there weren't any wars going on during his three years in the army. Korea was over and Vietnam hadn’t started yet.

Chapter 2

A few years passed and I bumped into Skeeter again. We had a good long talk about the good old days. He said when he got out of the Army he might get a job with the railroad. Two of his brothers were already working there. He was the same old Skeeter, happy-go-lucky as ever.

Durand was the next town over from Byron. It was a hub for the Grand Trunk Railroad. There were railroad tracks all over the place. You couldn't go through Durand without crossing tracks. The school's mascot was a train. They were called the Durand Railroaders.

Sure enough, when Skeeter got out of the Army he went to work for the Grand Trunk Railroad. He was a laborer at the railroad. He repaired and put down new tracks. These guys were called gandy dancers. They even had a song about the gandy dancers. It went something like this:

Oh, they danced on the ceiling,
and they danced on the wall
at the gandy dancers' ball.

Skeeter worked hard, drank hard, and fought hard, like the typical gandy dancer.

A short time later Skeeter did what most young men do. He met a pretty girl, got married, and started a family. Skeeter and his wife, Mary Lou, had five children, three boys, and two girls.

Chapter 3

Skeeter was a good hard worker and it paid off. He became a straw boss, sort of a crew leader which meant a little less work and more money. Time passed as time does. The railroad didn't change much and Durand stayed pretty much the same.

Except one thing did change. Drugs moved into town. It happens to all towns big and small. In the smaller towns, like Durand, people knew who was taking drugs and who was selling them.

Unfortunately, Skeeter's oldest boy was on drugs and big time. Skeeter did his best to get the boy to stop, but nothing seemed to work.

Skeeter's son died of an overdose.

Skeeter was devastated. His oldest child, his name's sake, Grant Junior dead at seventeen years old.

Skeeter was already a pretty heavy drinker. Now the drinking became worse. His favorite watering hole was the 602 Bar, which was a small, friendly bar where a lot of the railroaders hung out, drank beer, shot pool, and threw darts.

After his son's death, Skeeter didn't take part in the games as much, he just drank. He looked terrible. His eyes were bloodshot; he lost weight and looked more like a skeleton than a person. His disposition became unbearable making him hard to get along with at home, at work, and in the bar. Many nights Skeeter was escorted to the door of the 602 and told to go home.

He was no better at home. He would just continue drinking and fighting with Mary Lou. At work, Skeeter started showing up late or missing work altogether. He began drinking on the job and fighting with guys at work. Everybody knew Skeeter had problems, and people tried to be patient considering what he and the family had gone through, but it was becoming almost intolerable to have him around. Skeeter wasn't coping well, that much was obvious.

In one of his more sober moments, Skeeter decided to find out who was selling the drugs to his son. Everybody else already knew.

When Skeeter found out he made an appointment to see the Chief of Police, Ryan Berger. Chief Berger had been with the Durand Police for over twenty years.

When Skeeter entered the chief's office, Berger said, "Sit down, Skeeter." Chief Berger knew who Skeeter was, having been called several times to the 602 Bar where Skeeter was having a rather physical difference of opinion with one of

the patrons. “What’s on your mind?” Berger pretty much knew it had something to do with Skeeter's son's death.

Skeeter just stood in front of the chief's desk, hands at his side. He was exhausted, his hair was messier than usual, he looked ten years older than his years, and his eyes were bloodshot from drinking most of the night thinking of his dead son and how he died. In a low and steady voice, Skeeter said, “I know who killed my son. It was that fat stinking slob that hangs out at the 602 Bar, Tom Anderson.”

Berger looked up at Skeeter and said, “We know, Skeeter, we know.” Chief Berger also knew that Skeeter's son had been a user.

Skeeter slammed his fist on the chief desk and screamed, “Why haven’t you arrested him and put him in jail? What’s the matter with you?”

Rocking back in his chair Berger answered calmly, “We can’t prove anything. Can’t get enough evidence, no one will step up and testify.” He motioned to a chair and said again, “Have a seat, Skeeter. Let me try to explain.” The chief went on, “The police have been working undercover here in Durand and other cities all over the county and all over the state trying to get enough evidence on guys like Anderson. The drug dealers know it. No one will testify because the dealers and pushers are connected.”

Skeeter slumped into a chair. “What do you mean ‘connected’?”

Berger leaned forward. “The local pushers and dealers are just pee-ons. They work for organized crime in Detroit, Chicago, New York. Who knows where?”

"Who cares where they're from?"

Berger jumped up and shouted, "It doesn't matter where they're from! These are the big boys who will have your legs broken, or worse yet, kill anyone who would testify against even the lowest person in the drug chain. They won't let anyone mess with their organization."

Skeeter just sat in the chair looking down. "So what can we do?"

Berger walked over to Skeeter, put his hand on Skeeter's shoulder, and said, "Wait. Just wait for Anderson to make a mistake. And he will."

Skeeter got up from his chair and walked slowly out of the police chief's office, his usual quick and pleasant smile gone.

Chapter 4

After the visit with the chief, Skeeter's drinking became even worse. He had not been to work since the visit with Chief Berger. His fighting with Mary Lou grew worse.

After many days and nights of self-torture, Skeeter came up with the answer. He called the 602 Bar.

Mike, the bartender, answered the phone, “602.”

Skeeter asked, “Is Tom Anderson there?”

“Sure, want to talk to him?”

Skeeter hung up the phone.

It was just a few minutes past midnight. Skeeter put on his ball hat, coat, and work boots. He walked to the garage, got in his car, and drove seven miles to Durand and the 602 Bar.

At twelve-fifteen on a cool mid-October night, Skeeter entered the 602 Bar and walked over to the table where Tom Anderson and two of his cronies, Bill Barns and Toby Hicks,

were sitting. Anderson sat with his back to the wall so he could see everyone coming and going, no one was at his back. Barns sat to his right, Hicks to his left. All three men were armed with pistols. Barns and Hicks had their weapons tucked in the back of their trousers. The pistols were concealed by the jackets they wore. Anderson carried his pistol in the front right pocket. It was a little .38; he called it his pea shooter.

Anderson was the supplier; he recruited the pushers and obtained the drugs to sell. He was a fat man in his early thirties with a long scruffy beard and he always had a fiendish grin on his face. He dressed as if he were someone important. The look just didn't work. He wore a white long sleeve shirt that needed ironing, the same black-tie day after day. His huge belly flopped well over his belt holding up his worn khaki trousers. He had an air about him saying *I am the man! I'm the drug dealer neither the police nor anyone else can touch.*

Barns and Hicks were thought to be the pushers, the ones who sold the drugs to the kids. They had a good business selling to school kids from as young as seventh grade to high school seniors. Barns was much younger than Anderson, he was around twenty, nice looking. He acted and conducted himself like the young people he sold drugs to. He was able to lure them in. Hicks was a little older than Barns, at twenty-eight but not as well-groomed. He intimidated the kids when Barns' luring didn't work.

The three of them had been drunk most of the night and were, you might say, three sheets to the wind. The other eight patrons in the bar all knew that Anderson and his sidekicks were the drug dealers in Durand and the surrounding area. They may

have also had relatives on drugs, but they were all too afraid to say anything to the police. They all kept their distance from the trio.

The bar was dark, the music was loud, and everyone was having a good time in spite of Anderson and his boys.

Skeeter moved swiftly toward Anderson's table. At his right side, Skeeter was carrying a sawed-off twelve-gauge double-barrel shotgun loaded with double-ought buckshot. He had concealed the shotgun by putting the stock and most of the barrel up the sleeve of his jacket. No one paid any attention to Skeeter; he was a regular fixture at the 602, and lately, they didn't want anything to do with him because of his nasty disposition.

When Skeeter got within eight feet of Anderson he lifted the double-barrel shotgun and quietly said, "No more, no more." His heart was pounding fast, his hands were sweaty and all he could think of was *this is the man who sold drugs to my son*. He shot Tom Anderson in the head. Tom was blown back against the wall. He stuck there. Blood was everywhere. The force of the twelve-gauge blew Anderson's face beyond recognition. Pieces of his face clung to the wall and ceiling.

Just to drive his point home Skeeter gave ole Tom a blast from the second barrel. At which point Tom fell out of his chair with one less head.

Skeeter averted his attention to Barns and Hicks. They were petrified as were the other patrons in the bar. Time stood still. No one moved including Barns and Hicks. Turning slightly to his right, Skeeter pulled out a six-shot .38-caliber revolver that

he had tucked inside the front of his trousers and shot both Barns and Hicks, as Skeeter would say, right between the lookers.

The .38 made a small hole in the front but a big hole in the back. Blood and parts of the skull of both Barns and Hicks shot across the room. Skeeter's hands were sweating and shaking ever so slightly. His mouth seemed dry as if he had a mouth full of cotton. As he moved slowly backward Skeeter felt strangely calm, his heart rate returning to normal. The 602 Bar was normally loud with laughter, conversation, and music blaring from the jukebox, but now only Elvis sang "Don't Be Cruel" to a silent, gruesome room.

As Skeeter walked to the door, he could sense the other people in the room. When he reached the door, he said in a soft voice to the patrons who were still frozen in place, "Don't any of you move until I leave the bar. Don't even stick your head out the door. Just call the police and sit here." And he left.

Everyone in the bar was in total shock gazing at poor ole headless Tom and his two cronies lying on the floor, their blood and body parts still hanging on the wall and ceiling.

Slowly, Mike picked up the phone and called the police.

"Durand Police Department."

Mike, eerily calm, replied, "You better have someone come to the 602 Bar. Skeeter Jones just shot Tom Anderson and his two buddies."

Within ten minutes Officer Pete Miller entered the 602 Bar and said to himself, "Couldn't happen to three more deserving people." He turned and spoke to the patrons in the bar. "Don't anyone leave. We'll need to take statements from all of

you." He walked over to the bar and said, "Did you see the whole thing, Mike?"

Mike nodded and whispered, "Yes."

"Tell me about what happened here."

"Well, Pete, there's not much to tell. Skeeter came in carrying a double-barrel shotgun, walked over to where the three of them were sitting, and well, Skeeter shot Anderson twice in the head with the shotgun then pulled out a pistol and shot the other two in the head, once each."

Officer Miller ran a hand over his stubbled face. "I better call the chief. He's not going to like being woke up at twelve-thirty at night."

After fifteen rings, the chief's gravelly voice answered, "What's going on?"

"Skeeter Jones just shot and killed Tom Anderson and his two buddies Bill Barns and Toby Hicks."

Chief Berger, fully awake now, said, "It's about time somebody did. Call the state police. Tell them what happened. Don't let anyone leave the bar. I'll be right there."

After hanging up the phone, Miller walked toward the three dead men. He was not prepared for this. There was blood, bone, and brain matter splattered everywhere. The smell made his stomach lurch. He quickly looked away. He saw the people in the bar. Some were crying, some had their heads down, no one could look at the scene, but they would see it forever.

A few minutes later Chief Berger entered the bar. He walked to the scene and said, "I haven't seen anything like this since Vietnam."

About that same time, Michigan State Police Officer Bill Blankenship arrived. He was officially taking over this investigation.

Lieutenant Blankenship was a forty-five-year-old nice-looking man with fifteen years on the Michigan State Police force. He was a no-nonsense person, a "give me the facts ma'am, nothing but the facts" kind of guy. He had been called to investigate a homicide but was not expecting the scene before him.

"Helluva mess," Blankenship whispered, blowing out air and brushing a hand over his face. Though he had witnessed many murder scenes, it was not something he ever got used to.

Blankenship recovered his composure and professionalism then asked Berger, who knew his town and people best, to give him the who, what, where, and when of the crime. And the possible why.

Blankenship was well aware of the notorious Mr. Anderson and his two sidekicks. He asked Berger and Miller, "Where do you think Mr. Jones is now?"

Berger and Miller looked at each other and with a shrug of the shoulders the chief said, "We don't have a clue."

Lieutenant Blankenship probed, "Do you know where he lives?"

Berger answered, "Sure. Skeeter lives about a mile north out of Byron on New Lothrop Road."

Blankenship, with notepad and pencil in hand, asked, "Is there a Mrs. Jones?"

Both Berger and Miller nodded yes without saying a word. Miller then added, "And four kids."

"Which of you knows Mrs. Jones the best?"

"Well, I guess I do. Don't know her well, but I do know her," Miller offered.

"What's her name?"

"Mary, Mary Lou."

Lieutenant Blankenship turned to Chief Berger, "If it's alright with you, Chief, I would like Officer Miller to accompany me to check out Mr. Jones' home and inform his wife as to the events of the night. I would appreciate it if you'd stay here and conduct the rest of the investigation." Berger nodded his head.

Lieutenant Blankenship and Officer Miller left the bar and headed toward Skeeter's house.

Once there, Officer Miller knocked several times on the door. Mary Lou answered the door sleepy-eyed in her robe and slippers. Before she could say anything, Miller removed his hat and apologetically asked if they could come in. She nodded. Both men entered the house at 1666 New Lothrop Road.

Officer Miller began, "Mary Lou, I've got some really bad news to tell you." She opened her mouth to speak, but before she could say a word, he went on, "Skeeter shot and killed Tom Anderson and his two buddies at the 602 Bar."

Mary Lou fell to her knees with her face in her hands and started sobbing. "I knew he was going to do something like this."

Miller knelt down and helped Mary Lou to a chair in the living room. She kept repeating the same thing. "I just knew he would do it, I just knew it."

With no hint of empathy, Blankenship asked, "Mrs. Jones, do you know where your husband is, or where he might be? It would be better for all concerned if we find him soon."

"No, I have no idea where he is."

"When was the last time you saw your husband?"

Mary Lou took a long minute to collect her thoughts. With a shaky breath, she finally replied, "I don't know exactly. About midnight. We had been arguing most of the night about this drug thing. That's all we've done lately is argue and fight over the death of our son and the drugs and dealers behind it."

"Mrs. Jones, does your husband have any guns stored in the house?"

Mary Lou gave a sarcastic chuckle, "He has dozens of guns, you know that, Pete." Addressing Blankenship she said, "They're all in a safe out in the garage away from the kids."

Blankenship was getting tired of being patient, "Do you mind if we look around? It's just standard procedure."

Mary Lou motioned in the direction of the garage and said, "Sure, go ahead. Let me get you the key to the gun cabinet." Mary Lou went to the bedroom and found the key in the bottom of Skeeter's sock drawer. It was still there. This small thing made Mary Lou feel some relief.

She came back to the room where the two policemen were waiting and handed the key to Lieutenant Blankenship. However, he was not interested in Skeeter's gun collection; he was really wondering if Mary Lou might be hiding Skeeter.

After making a thorough investigation of the house, basement, and garage Blankenship reentered the house and walked over to Mary Lou and said, "Thank you for your

cooperation. If you see or hear from your husband, please call," as he handed her a business card. Then added, "If there is anything I can do, please let me know."

"That goes for me, too. Anything you need, give me or my wife a call," Miller said.

Blankenship and Miller left the house and headed for Durand. On the way, Miller said, "Quite a mess Skeeter got himself into."

Blankenship nodded, "More than you might think. If we get to him first he will go to prison for life. If the mob gets to him they will beat him half to death then shoot him."

Skeeter exited the bar, got into his car, and paused for a few seconds. He looked at his hand and noticed it shaking again, his pulse increased. Reality started to sink in. He put the car in gear and headed west, crossing several railroad tracks, and left the city limits of Durand heading toward Byron. A mile or so out of Durand, Skeeter, for no good reason, turned onto Prior Road and began to slow down.

About a half-mile down the road he came to a single set of railroad tracks running north and south. Seeing these made Skeeter remember working on the tracks, replacing some of the railroad ties, back when times were good.

Just before he crossed the tracks, he noticed a lane leading into a farmer's field. Skeeter drove onto the lane. To his left, between the railroad tracks and the farmer's field, was a small piece of land covered with an overgrowth of shrubs, bushes, and small trees. Skeeter pulled into the overgrowth concealing his car from the road. He shut the engine off, let his

head fall back, and said in a loud agonizing voice, "What have I done, what have I done?"

~~~~~~

Well, I'll tell you what you've done, Skeeter. You blew the head off ole Tom Anderson and put a bullet between the eyes of both Barns and Hicks, and left your wife with a house full of kids. The Durand, county, and state police are all after you, and oh, let's not forget about the mob. They'll be after you too. That's what you have done.

~~~~~~

Somewhere along the line, I lost track of Skeeter, But I can tell you one thing, the people back in Durand didn't blame Skeeter for blowing away Tom Anderson and his boys. They were rotten through and through. There was a half-hearted investigation that faded out over time. Everybody wondered *Whatever happened to ole Skeeter?* Did the mob catch up with him and bury him next to Hoffa? Did he ride the rails, or did he just wander off into no man's land and do unto himself as he did unto Anderson?

Chapter 5

Skeeter sat in his car concealed among the overgrowth of shrubs, bushes, and small trees wondering about the recent turn of events. His thoughts were whirling around in his head. It all felt so surreal. Skeeter had made no plans for what to do after he shot the three men. No plan B. He knew he had to do something but didn't know what.

Skeeter got out of his car leaving his sawed off shotgun on the front seat and looked at his surroundings. He knew he couldn't keep driving his car. They would locate it and him in no time. The only thing left to do was start walking. He headed toward a slight incline leading to the railroad tracks, but then remembered the old duffel bag he kept in the trunk in case of emergencies.

Skeeter fumbled with his keys in the moonlight muttering curses at his key ring. After several tries, he finally got the trunk open. He felt around the dark trunk and was about to

give up thinking Mary Lou had maybe taken it out when his hand felt the canvas bag shoved way to the back.

He pulled the duffel bag out and unzipped it. In the dim light of the moon, he could see it held a worn army blanket, a small first aid kit, and a flashlight with dead batteries. Dusty as it was, he was thankful it was still there.

Somehow the duffel bag gave him a small sense of confidence. Before he shut the trunk, he threw his keys inside and headed back up the incline to the tracks.

Standing in the middle of the railroad tracks he looked north in the direction of Durand. He knew he couldn't go back; he just couldn't do the time in prison. He would go crazy locked up. Worse yet he didn't want the mob to get hold of him. So south it was.

Dressed in blue jeans, heavy plaid shirt, warm jacket, and baseball cap, with a half pack of cigarettes, and of course, his .38 tucked neatly in the front of his trousers, he was ready for the cool October night and what might lie ahead.

Skeeter walked slowly for half an hour while thinking of his past. His mind was a mess. Of course, he thought about the shooting, but more than that he thought of his wife, family, his job, and friends. The good times shooting pool at the 602 Bar. And of course, the ever-present question: *What am I going to do?* Just as soon as one thought entered his head another would overtake it. But that's all they were - thoughts. He knew he should feel miserable or remorse for what he did, but he didn't at this moment. He only felt numb.

Just as he dropped his cigarette to put it out Skeeter saw a small flash of light coming from under the trestle ahead of him.

His heart started to pound. *Could that be the light from a policeman's flashlight? Did they discover my car already? Have they started a manhunt for me?* He told himself it wasn't the police because there was only one light. He would have expected many more searchlights and voices, but right now all was silent. Skeeter started to calm down and collect his thoughts. He decided to continue on his journey to nowhere. After a few steps, he changed his mind. He wondered what the light was, if not from a flashlight, then what? He needed to know if anyone saw him. He bent slightly forward, eyes wide open fighting to see through the moonlit night. He stepped off the tracks and started walking down the slope toward the light.

Suddenly he recognized where he was. He remembered just ahead of him was a creek that flowed under a trestle. The stream was about fifteen feet wide and one to two feet deep. Skeeter remembered this area from his gandy dancer days working on the railroad. He spent many a day riding a trolley car up and down the tracks between Durand and Byron.

He carefully walked closer to the light, his eyes moving quickly back and forth looking for who knows what. It was a campfire. His eyes strained to see. He couldn't imagine what a fire was doing here. Over the fire was what appeared to be a pot of coffee. He couldn't see anything or anyone else.

Suddenly from out of the darkness, he heard a voice. "It's chilly tonight. Would you like to come sit by the fire? I have a pot of coffee brewing. It's not very good but it's hot." The man behind the voice was a lonely hobo hoping for a friend.

Skeeter jumped back, almost falling down. He pulled out the .38 revolver he had tucked in his trousers. His eyes darted

back and forth in the direction of the voice. Nothing. He couldn't see anyone.

Again the voice. "Are you going to shoot me or have a cup of coffee?" From out of the darkness a man appeared. His clothes looked worn and dirty. He had a well-worn fedora with a hole in the front. He was smoking a pipe that he kept in his mouth while he was talking. It bobbed up and down as he spoke. He said, "What will it be?" The man turned and started walking to the campfire.

Skeeter dropped his hand holding the pistol to his side and followed the man. Skeeter's head was pounding. *What am I doing following some old hobo? I should be worried about the police and the mob.*

"Here," the man pointed toward the fire, "have a seat." Looking at the pistol in Skeeter's hand, he said, "Put that thing away, it makes me nervous."

Skeeter put the .38 back in his trousers.

The man smiled and said, "That's better." He poured some coffee into what looked like an old Campbell's Soup can. Skeeter took a sip and thought *He's right. It tastes terrible, but it's hot.*

The man, looking at the fire and poking it with a stick said, "Did you kill somebody?"

Skeeter, startled, titled back and said, "Why would you ask that?"

The man turned and looked at Skeeter and said, "Well, let's see, it's the middle of the night, we're in the woods, and you have a pistol in your hand. What do you want me to think? You

just decided to leave your house and take a walk, meet up with me, and have a cup of coffee?"

Skeeter leaned forward and said matter of factly, "Yeah, you're right, I killed somebody. Three somebodies." He was shocked to hear his own voice. Saying the words and hearing them come back to him suddenly made it true.

"Did you kill all three tonight?"

"All three. Bang, bang, bang." It felt like it was someone else speaking as Skeeter admitted his deeds. He felt relieved to say it out loud. "Yes, I killed someone." The magnitude of what he'd done was sinking in.

"Want to tell me about it? Everyone has a story to tell. Might do you some good to get it off your chest?"

Skeeter was drained physically and emotionally. He didn't have any idea what his next move should be. He didn't know where he was going or how to get there. He needed help and this hobo might be the only hope he had. Skeeter dropped his head in an almost prayerful posture. Very slowly Skeeter started to tell how he shot Tom Anderson's head off with a twelve-gauge and then shot Barns and Hicks. The whole story. As he continued to talk the information began pouring out more freely about the drugs. How his son died of an overdose, his wife and his kids, the job on the railroad. Everything. Skeeter felt comfortable talking to this hobo for some reason. Skeeter sensed something about this man. Although dressed like a hobo and needing a shave, there was something that just didn't fit.

A half-hour later Skeeter was finally done. The man simply said, "Wow! That's some story."

"You said everyone has a story. What's yours?"

The man stood and walked toward Skeeter with his hand out and said, “My name is Dr. C. William Palmer, M.D. My friends call me Palmer. What’s yours?”

Skeeter, startled by the *I am Dr. C. William Palmer, M.D.*, said, “I’m Skeeter Jones. My friends call me Skeeter. Are you really a doctor?”

“Yes, I am a doctor. Your parents really named you Skeeter?”

“No, they named me Grant. I go by Skeeter. I’m not sure how I got the nickname. They say when I was little I would curse out the mosquitoes for biting me and I called them skeeters. I told you my story, now you tell me yours.”

Palmer walked back to the stump he had been sitting on and gazed into the fire before saying, “Yep, I am, or was, a real doctor. A family doctor in a small town just outside Pittsburgh, son of a steelworker who was the son of a steelworker. Almost all my family worked in the mills in the Pittsburgh area. Some, like you, worked for the railroad. Hardworking, honest people. Then I came along. Dr. C. William Palmer, M.D. How proud they all were! Steelworker’s kid becomes a doctor. Then they weren’t so proud,” Palmer stopped talking and dropped his head.

“What happened?”

“I was leading the good life. Wife, kids, three of them, two boys and a girl. Nice house, two cars, place on a lake, and a boat, even had a dog named Spot. The whole nine yards. Perfect. Belonged to the Rotary Club. Was having a great time. Partying, drinking a little, then drinking a lot more. Doing a little drugs. A snort here and a snort there. Just a little, not bad. I wasn’t a drunk or a drug addict. I started noticing women a little more.

Booze, drugs, and women are not a good mix when you're supposed to be the straight and narrow doctor that everybody knows and trusts. Not when you're the doctor in a small town of hardworking, honest people. My wife was putting up with the booze pretty well, she was not aware of the drugs. But when it came to the women she had enough and divorced me. She took everything. The house, car, place at the lake, kids, money, even the dog. Everything. I lost my medical practice. She even sold that. As it turns out nobody wants a drunk, druggie, and woman-chaser for a doctor. After a few weeks of more drinking, drugs, and feeling sorry for myself I decided to contact a colleague I knew from medical school, Dr. Paul Philips, and start over again."

After a short pause, Skeeter asked, "What happened. Did it work?"

"Well, I'm here aren't I? Of course, it didn't work. I drank more and did more drugs. I was a real mess. Paul, Dr. Philips, just couldn't keep me around. I moved out of my low-end apartment and moved into a real dump on the so-called bad side of town, right into the outskirts of the city, and drank myself into some sort of coma. After some time I woke up, laid around a while trying to think of what to do next. I had no ability to make money other than being a doctor and that was out of the question. I thought about suicide but didn't want to bring even more shame to my family than I already had. The truth is I didn't have the guts to put a gun to my head and pull the trigger. I got up one morning, put on some clothes, put some personal things into a small duffel bag, and decided to leave my small dumpy apartment.

"When I left the apartment building I walked to a nearby railroad track and stood in the middle of them. I looked one way then I looked the other and asked myself which way to go. To my left, a few blocks away, was a steel mill and the inner city, and to my right, almost running through my apartment were several sets of railroad tracks running to somewhere. Guess which way I went. I didn't have the slightest idea what to do. I just started walking. I don't know how long or how far I walked. The longer I walked the slower I walked.

"After what seemed an eternity I heard a voice. I knew it wasn't God because the voice said, 'Where the hell are you going?' Startled, I started looking around. The voice came again. This time it said, 'Over here, stupid, in the woods.' I looked in the direction of the woods and started walking. In just a short distance I saw the person behind the voice. A short grubby little man dressed even worse than me. He had a beat-up old fedora on his head with a full scrubby beard that was dark and white in color. If he would have had his teeth missing you might have thought he was Gabby Hayes out of the old cowboy movies of the past. He asked me if I was hungry. I nodded. Until then I hadn't thought much about eating, but all of a sudden I was starving. He told me to come with him, and we walked a few yards into the woods and there was his camp. Very similar to the one I have here. He served something he called soup and something else he called coffee. We swapped stories about how we got to where we were. Finally, he said, 'My name is Ted. What's yours?' I told him and asked what his last name was. He told me he didn't use one. To this day I still don't know his last name. He told me I needed to decide where I was going because

going back wasn't an option. He said I could team up with him and he'd show me the ropes. I decided sure, why not, and chose to go with him. I will always remember how Ted took me under his wing and said, 'Welcome aboard, partner!' We shook hands and traveled for the better part of three years together. Ted taught me everything I know about being a hobo."

Complctcly absorbed in Palmer's story, Skeeter asked, "What happened? Where's Ted now?"

Palmer sat there a moment poking at the fire with a stick. Finally, he looked at Skeeter and said, "Dead. Woke up one morning and old Ted was dead. I have been a little lonely the past couple of years without him." Then he looked at Skeeter, "Tell you what I'll do. I'll make the same offer to you Ted made me. If you decide to run the rails I will teach you the ropes. Everything you need to know. It might even save your life. Running the rails can be very dangerous if you don't know what you're doing."

Without hesitating, Skeeter said, "Sure, why not?"

They shook hands and Palmer said, "Welcome aboard, partner," just like old Ted said to him.

Putting more wood on the fire, Palmer said, "Remember, you can't trust anyone. The other hobos will kill you for fifty cents. By the way, how much money you got?"

Skeeter pulled out his billfold, "Oh about..."

"Didn't I just say you can't trust anyone? I mean anyone. Well, you can trust me. Take whatever money you have and put it in your shoe. Don't let anyone know where it is."

Skeeter removed his left shoe and put all the money he had in it, forty-one dollars and change, and put the shoe back on.

Palmer said again with a smile, "Didn't I just say don't let anyone know where you hide your money?" They both had a good laugh. Now with a very serious look, Palmer said, "They really will cut your throat for fifty cents or less." Skeeter got the idea.

Doc said, "It's late, you need some sleep." Skeeter was grateful to have someone who wasn't looking to kill him. He found a relatively bump-free area on the ground and pulled his blanket out of his duffel bag, giving it a good shake before covering up. Before long he was sound asleep.

Next thing Skeeter knew something or somebody was tapping the bottom of his foot. It was Palmer. "We got to get on the road before somebody finds you."

Skeeter opened his eyes and sat up in wonderment thinking *Where am I*? For a moment he thought it was a dream but just as quickly he remembered and said to himself *It wasn't just a dream, I really did kill three people.*

"Come on, we gotta get going. No time for coffee."

Skeeter was baffled, "But it's the middle of the night!"

"No," Palmer corrected, "it's early morning. It's maybe five or five-thirty. Come on, let's go. The police are surely looking for you. It won't be long before they find your car and start looking up and down the tracks."

Palmer and Skeeter packed up what belongings they had, then Palmer spread the ashes from the fire around. After Palmer was done with his housekeeping, you couldn't tell anyone had been there.

In a few minutes, they were on the tracks heading south. The time was six A.M.

Chapter 6

At ten A.M. Kevin Matthews was turning east off Durand Road onto Prior Road heading toward his mother's house. He was going to take her to her doctor's appointment.

A hundred or so feet before he crossed the railroad tracks that Skeeter and Palmer were walking on, Kevin saw a flash of light coming from the overgrowth between the tracks and the farmer's field. He saw the light reflected from a car's rear window and immediately wondered if someone had an accident and could still be in the car. There didn't appear to be any skidmarks. He slowed down and noticed a lane leading to the farmer's field. He pulled in and shut the engine off. He got out and walked cautiously into the brush. The car was deep in the underbrush but he thought it wasn't driven there by accident. Kevin parked in the lane and walked the short distance to the car in the brush. He peered through the window to see if someone

was injured in the car. He didn't see anyone or anything unusual in the car. He did have, however, the presence of mind to write down the make and model of the car along with the license plate number.

Something was just not right about this. Kevin had not turned on his television or radio that morning to hear the news of the killings at the 602 Bar.

He got back into his car and drove to his mother's house. Once inside he said to his mother, "Guess what I just saw?"

Before his mother, Janet could say anything he answered his own question, "A car in the brush along the railroad tracks just down the road. It was deep in the brush, I knew something had to be wrong. Maybe an accident but it wasn't."

Janet said with a start, "Was anyone hurt?"

"No. Nobody there. The car was empty."

"What kind of car was it? What color was it?"

Kevin took out his slip of paper he'd written the car's details on, "It was an older Ford. I'm not good at knowing the years of cars anymore. It was an older Ford. Black. What difference does it make?"

"Didn't you hear? It's all over the T.V.," Janet was getting agitated recalling the news and her son's limited knowledge.

"What's all over the T.V.?"

"The killings at the bar in Durand!"

"What killings, what bar?" Kevin was mildly interested as he peered in the refrigerator for something to eat.

Janet was approaching fever pitch. "I don't know what bar! The 605 or 702. I don't know which bar! Some guy shot and

killed three or four people. It sounds like the car he might have been driving is the car you saw at the tracks! They said it was a black Ford. You should give the police a call!"

"Did they say who did the shooting?" Kevin asked while biting into an apple.

"Some guy that worked on the railroad. Skeet, Scat. Something like that."

At this information, Kevin halted mid-chew and said, "Skeeter, Skeeter Jones!"

"Yeah. That sounds about right. Did you know him?"

Kevin now lost all interest in eating, "Shoot pool with him once in a while at the 602."

Janet who had begun to relax now began to fuss again, "I told you you shouldn't be hanging around places like that! Do you think you should give the police a call?"

"Might not be the car they're looking for," Kevin answered thinking about his pool shooting acquaintance.

"It's a car that parked off the road into the brush alongside a railroad track the night a man kills three people at a nearby bar! That sounds mighty suspicious! Should be enough to call the police, if you ask me."

"When you put it like that, guess you're right."

Kevin picked up the phone and called the Shiawassee County Sheriff's office.

By now they had been informed by the Michigan State Police in Owosso of the crimes committed at the 602 Bar in Durand.

Chapter 7

DOUBTFUL

"Shiawassee County dispatch. What is your emergency?"

"I think I found the car you're looking for in connection with the killings in Durand."

The dispatcher's nasally voice came back quickly, "What's your name?"

"My name is Kevin Matthews."

"Just a moment. I will connect you to the sheriff."

Sheriff Richard Curts was a rather portly man of medium height in his late fifties. He had been a member of the Shiawassee County Police Department for twenty-seven years, the last five as Sheriff. While serving as a patrolman he earned a degree in criminal justice. He then served six years as Under Sheriff, number two man in the county sheriff's department. He had a rough manner about him but was a kind and caring person.

He ran the department informally and was on a first name basis with his staff.

"Sheriff, I have Mr. Kevin Matthews on the line. He says he thinks he found Skeeter Jones' car."

"Put him through."

The dispatcher connected the sheriff and Kevin in a split second. "Hello. This is Sheriff Curts. I understand you have some potential evidence in the killing at the 602."

Kevin croaked out a slow, nervous, "Yes, hello sir, my name is Kevin Matthews. I live just south of Durand at 1875 east Prior Road." He was still nervous but hit his stride, "I was going to my mother's house. She lives on west Prior Road. Well, I was going there to take her to the doctor. The doctor's office is in Owosso. She is old and has trouble with arthritis and..."

"Yes. I'm sorry to hear that, but could you tell me about the car you found? Where did you find it? Do you know the make and model?"

"Oh yeah. Sorry. It's an older Ford, black or dark blue. I've got the license number too, it's XUY 994."

Sheriff Curts looked over the information the state police discussed with him and noticed the license number was a perfect match to Skeeter's car. Without divulging this knowledge to Kevin, Sheriff Curts thanked him for the information and said, "You have been a great help."

Kevin, in a very anxious voice, said, "Is it Skeeter's car? Do you know where he is?"

Curts said, "I'm not positive at this point. Thank you again for your help," and hung up.

The sheriff called the dispatcher and asked, “Who is patrolling the southeast corner of the county?”

“That would be Steve Harron, Sheriff.”

“We have only one officer covering half the entire county? So much for keeping the sixty thousand residents safe and secure. Patch him through to my office phone, please.”

The dispatcher, using protocol called Officer Harron, “Steve, the sheriff wants to talk to you. I’ll patch you through.”

Within moments the dispatcher had the officer on the phone, “Sheriff, Officer Harron is on the line.”

“Steve, I want you to go ASAP to the railroad crossing on Prior Road between Byron and Durand Roads. I have reason to believe that Skeeter Jones' car is parked on the east side of the tracks. Secure the area. Don’t let anyone near the car. Wait for me to get there.”

Officer Harron responded, “I’m on my way. I am about fifteen minutes out.”

“I will see you there.”

The sheriff paged his secretary, Norma.

“Yes, sheriff.”

“Norma, get me Lieutenant Blankenship at the state police post in Owosso.”

A moment later Sheriff Curts was speaking with Blankenship. “We have a lead on the Skeeter Jones case.”

“What do you have?”

The sheriff told Blankenship about the interview with Kevin Matthews. “Can you meet me at the railroad crossing on Prior Road between Durand and Byron Road?”

“I'll be there in thirty minutes.”

Curts informed him, “I assigned Officer Steve Harron from the county to meet us there. I will see you there in thirty minutes.” He slammed the phone and rushed through the office pulling a too-small jacket over his bulk. Passing by his secretary's desk and grabbing a donut on his way, he called out, “If anybody wants me I will be at the railroad crossing on Prior between Durand and Byron Roads.

Fifteen minutes later Sheriff Curts was at the railroad crossing and saw Officer Steve Harron was at the scene.

The sheriff pulled onto the lane entering the farmer's field. He shut the engine off and proceeded to the car parked among the shrubs. He greeted office Harron with a sharp nod. Moments later Lieutenant Blankenship pulled into the lane with two people from the Michigan State Police Crime Lab, followed by four members of the K-9 unit along with four obedient but menacing German shepherds.

Sheriff Curts, Lieutenant Blankenship, and Officer Harron walked up the slight hill leading to the tracks. Looking up and down the single set of tracks, Curts spoke to no one in particular, “Which way did he go? North? Not likely. That’s where he came from, where he committed the crime. Naw, I'd say he went south.”

Harron asked, “Why south? What’s there?”

“Nothing. That’s where he wants to be.”

Blankenship added, “Going south is everywhere. Indiana, Ohio, Illinois, and beyond. It’s just about noon. He’s had a twelve-hour start. If he’s on foot he could be a few miles down the tracks, if he jumped a train he could be a hundred to two hundred miles away. We need to expand the search. I’ll

make a statewide A.P.B. and ask the Ohio, Indiana, and Illinois State Police for help at the border. We'll have the state police helicopter make a few passes up and down the tracks. I'll also get the Grand Trunk Railroad involved. Maybe their people can spot him on the tracks."

Chapter 8

HALT

At six A.M. Skeeter and Palmer just started on their journey south. Both of them thinking to themselves.

Palmer was thinking *Poor slob. He just killed three people. Lost his family, lost his job. Has the police after him. Worse yet he has the mob after him. He really doesn't know where he is going or what to expect. He doesn't know if he can trust me. Why would he trust an old worn-out hobo like me?* With a smile on his face, Palmer thought it was nice to have someone to travel with, to have a friend like Ted.

Skeeter, on the other hand, was desperate. He was thinking *Where am I going? The police are after me. The mob probably. What's going to happen to my family? What are Mary Lou and the kids going to do? No money. My kids will have others calling them names and saying things like, 'Your father is a murderer!' How do I know if I can trust Palmer? He seems alright. He did say the rail runners will kill you for fifty cents.*

He has already given me survival information, a place to sleep, such as it was, and food, such as it was, and a real plan for the future. Such as it may be. Yes, I trust him. My life is in his hands. I have no other choice.

Chapter 9

The mob, organized crime, The Mafia. Whatever you want to call them, they are coming after Skeeter Jones. They cannot let one of their own be hurt let alone killed without someone paying for it. No matter how low on the chain. Someone will pay, and pay big.

If the mob gets to Skeeter before the police they will beat him to within an inch of his life, then squeeze the other inch until he is dead.

If the police catch up with Skeeter before the mob, they will arrest him and put him in jail. Charge him. He will go to trial. Be found guilty and be sentenced to prison for life. After which the mob will have him killed in prison.

The mob has connections everywhere. Especially in prison. Who do you think are in prisons, along with your assortment of murderers, bank robbers, and general bad guys? Of course drug dealers. There are all kinds of drugs being bought

and sold every day in every prison. They will put the finger on Skeeter and he's done. The mob will pay good money for someone on the inside to kill him.

It comes down to this: If the mob catches Skeeter, he’s dead. If the police catch him he’s dead.

Better keep moving down the line, Skeeter, put your trust in God and Dr. C. William Palmer, M.D.

Chapter 10

After walking for over two hours, Palmer said to Skeeter, "There is a small town of Byron ahead."

"Yeah, that's where I'm from. I can't go there, they'll recognize me!"

"OK, I'll go into town and get us something to eat. We will eat it on the go. Gotta keep ahead of everyone until we cross the state line."

Skeeter, not knowing exactly where they were headed yet blindly trusting Palmer to guide him, asked, "What state line?"

"Does it matter?

Although Skeeter had been fine not making any more life decisions, he answered, "I guess not, but I'd kinda like an idea where we're heading."

"Just past the railroad crossing that leads to town, there's an old, small train depot and old Western Union telegraph office that's not used anymore. On the other side of the tracks, there is a grain elevator. Just beyond that is where we are going to jump on a train. A few miles down the line we will come to a train station that has tracks running in all directions. Some will lead to Ohio, some to Indiana, some to Illinois, that's when we have to decide where we're going. I choose Indiana."

"Why Indiana?"

"Carny," was the only thing Palmer said like it was supposed to mean something.

"Carny? What do you mean 'carny'?"

"Carnival. You know what a carnival is, don't you?" Without waiting for a reply he said, "A great place to hide when you're running from something or someone. Carnivals and circuses are great places. I like carnivals best."

Skeeter's doubts about following Palmer were suddenly rekindled. Palmer saw Skeeter's worried expression and clarified, "They don't ask many questions when you go to work for them. You can make a little money, and I do mean *little* money. You get three hots and a cot. The meals aren't very good and the sleep arrangements aren't much better, but it's good for quick money when you're on the run."

"You worked at many carnivals?"

"Three or four. We'll try and catch up with Dobbs. I hear he's somewhere south of South Bend."

"Who's Dobbs?"

"Dobbs is the owner of Dobbs' Carnival. He is one of the more reputable carny owners. Most of the carny owners

don't treat people like you and me very well. They know we're on the run from somebody." Looking around wondering if they'd make the train in time, Palmer asked, "What time you got?"

Skeeter looked at his railroad pocket watch, the one that Mary Lou had given him for his first Christmas after hiring on the railroad. "It's three thirty-five."

"Our jump-off will be about four-thirty. There is a jungle about a mile from there."

Skeeter was getting more nervous about this hobo business. "What's a 'jungle'?"

Palmer laughed. "A jungle is a camp where hobos hang out, eat, sleep, tell stories. That's where we're going to find out where Dobbs is." With a smile and a shake of his head, Palmer said. "Boy, Skeeter, you got a lot to learn. Hobos have a language all their own. Hoboing is another world. Good thing you got me. You wouldn't last a day." Turning serious, Palmer went on, "When we get to the jungle from now on and for the rest of your life, you lie. You lie about everything. We need to change your name, where you're from, what you did for a living. There can be no trail to your past."

Skeeter could see that Palmer was right. If he was going to make it, he had to reinvent himself. While he was letting this sink in, Palmer was at work mulling over Skeeter's new identity. "Let's see, what would be a good name for you? You look like you could be an Andy, Andrew Anderson."

Shocked back to reality at Palmer's recommended name for him, Skeeter spat, "That's the last name of the drug dealer I blew the head off back in Durand. There is no way I will wear that name!"

Palmer backpedaled, “Okay. So that was a bad call. What about Miller? Andy Miller from South Bend, Indiana. Your line of work was construction. That sounds pretty generic. We don’t need to be too specific. There won’t be a lot of questions from the people you will be dealing with from now on anyway. Most of them lie about everything too.”

As Palmer and Skeeter approached the railroad intersection that leads to Byron, Palmer stopped, put his hand on Skeeter's shoulder, and said, “We’ll stop here, Skeeter. I’m going to cross over the tracks and go into town for some food. Remember me telling you about the Western Union stop? That’s it to the left,” Palmer said pointing, “and the grain elevator over to the right.” Skeeter nodded his head. He knows this area very well. He had lived in Byron most of his life. “I want you to cross the road until you get about halfway between the telegraph office and elevator. Make sure no one can see you. Jump over the fence and start walking between the elevator and the old Western Union Station. Once you’re past them a couple hundred feet, come back to the tracks. Lay down in the weeds. I will come and get you. We'll eat and jump on the next train.”

Palmer stretched out his hand and said, “Um, I’ll need some money. Can’t get much just on my good looks.”

Skeeter took off his left shoe and handed a twenty dollar bill to Palmer. “That should be enough.”

Now it was Palmer’s turn to be shocked, “We don’t want to buy the store! We just want some food. I haven’t seen that much money since I can’t remember when!”

Palmer put the money in his pocket, crossed over the road, and headed east toward town.

Skeeter put his shoe on, crossed the road, and started thinking to himself. *Am I ever going to see Palmer again or is he going to take his newfound treasure and move on?*

Skeeter walked looking both ways. He saw nothing, climbed over the short fence, and continued walking until he passed between the Western Union station and elevator. He walked slowly, almost crawling so the weeds would hide him. Every few feet he would look to see if anyone saw him. He was getting nervous, the telegraph office was closed but there was still some action at the elevator. After some time he was in the clear. He made a beeline for tracks and lay down in the weeds as Palmer told him to do.

Lying there in the weeds Skeeter looked up into the clear sky of a warm early October afternoon. He started remembering what it was like when he and his buddy Butch would lay on the bank of the ole Shiawassee River, their fishing poles stuck in the mud next to them, line in the water waiting to catch Mr. Big, an old largemouth bass that kept getting away. Not a care in the world. It was so peaceful, the two of them would often fall to sleep. He was so content in his thoughts, he nearly fell asleep right then.

A loud noise woke him. He sat up, heart beating, eyes wide open. It was only a bevy of birds flying out of some nearby trees. Then reality set in. His new life. The here and now. Running, hiding, jumping trains, lying, not knowing where the next meal would come from, where he'd sleep at night, or where money would come from. Oh yeah, then there's the mob.

A few minutes later Palmer showed up with a couple of sacks of hamburgers, French fries, coffee, and two cans of

vegetables. "Bet you thought I was going to skip out on you, didn't ya?

Palmer was smiling from ear to ear. He hadn't had a restaurant hamburger and fries in years. His hands were shaking as he handed one sack to Skeeter. "Eat up, eat up! This is going to be one of the best meals you're going to get for some time. We got to get ready to board the Grand Trunk heading south."

"I understand the hamburger, fries, and coffee, but what's with the vegetables?"

"Never know when you need vegetables." Palmer grinned without further explanation. "By the way, Skeeter, here's your change." Skeeter shrugged and put it in his shoe without counting it.

Skeeter caught Palmer's slip up by calling him Skeeter instead of Andy. "Who am I, Palmer? Skeeter Jones killer of three, husband, father, railroad worker from Durand? Or Andy Miller, a construction worker from South Bend, Indiana?" Skeeter was feeling frustrated and overwhelmed by his new identity.

"Skeeter when we're alone, Andy everywhere else. I hope I don't slip up and call you Skeeter when I should call you Andy or Andy when I should call you Skeeter. I'm confused already."

Palmer looked north down the tracks, saw the train coming. "Here she comes. Looks like she is a long one moving slow. Follow my lead. Do exactly what I do. We need to look for an open car that will make getting on easier."

As the train went slowly by, Palmer jumped to his feet like a cat, threw his bedroll in the car, ran along beside, put his

hands on the floor of the railroad car, and swung himself in. He immediately turned toward the open door of the boxcar and stretched out his hand. Skeeter, following close behind, did exactly as Palmer did. He threw his duffel bag in, grabbed Palmer's hand, and swung himself up. Skeeter hit the floor rolling over.

Palmer stood looking down at Skeeter sprawled on the floor of the boxcar flat on his back. "Not the smoothest entrance I've seen but not bad for a First of May guy."

"I'm not sure what the date is, I know it's not the first of May."

Laughing, Palmer said, "No, it's not the first of May. *You* are the First of May. First of May is hobo for tenderfoot, greenhorn, beginner. That's what you're going to be called for a while. Find a spot, lay down, and relax. We got about two more hours before we jump off. Then we'll walk a mile or so to the jungle where they might have some bullets or mulligan stew or maybe even cacklers."

Skeeter, slightly irritated, said, "Okay. Enough of the hobo lingo."

Palmer looking straight into Skeeter's eyes with a serious look on his face told him, "It's not a joke, Skeeter, you will need to learn it to survive."

"OK, I give, what are bullets, mulligan stew, and cacklers?" Skeeter asked, not really caring at this point.

"Bullets and 100 on a plate are beans, mulligan stew is beef stew, and cacklers are eggs. At least now you will be able to order breakfast and dinner at a jungle."

In a few minutes with the train wheels bump-bumping along, the boxcar slowly swaying back and forth, Skeeter was out like a light.

The next thing Skeeter knew Palmer was tapping on his foot. "Get up, it's time. The train is coming into the South Bend railroad station. We got to be careful. A lot of bulls around here. Know what I mean?"

Skeeter sat up, his hands on his knees. "Yeah, I know what bulls are. Cops."

"Get your stuff. The train will be moving real slow. Jump when I jump." Moving to the open door of the boxcar, both men held onto their worldly possessions in one bag the size of a pillowcase. Palmer glanced at Skeeter and he knew jumping off a moving train was a lot more difficult and dangerous than jumping on. There have been many a broken bone and even death from jumping off a moving train. Injury to a hobo is very serious. Hobos don't have Blue Cross. Palmer saw the fear on Skeeter's face. "When you jump, land on your feet then roll. You will be alright."

Skeeter was petrified. The train was not moving fast but to Skeeter, it was going a hundred miles an hour. All he could visualize were broken bones. Arms, legs, maybe a neck. He looked at Palmer.

Palmer, with a slight smile, said, "You're going to be just fine. When you jump, remember, jump feet first and bend your knees. When you hit the ground be sure to roll," Then he looked out the door and yelled, "Now!"

Both men jumped, rolled, and were up in one motion.

"Good job, Skeeter! Now let's move out."

"Yeah, piece of cake, nothing to it," as Skeeter looked around trying to find out which direction was up.

They started walking south. Forever south.

"We should be to the jungle in a couple of miles. Just about dinner time."

As they continued to walk on, Skeeter was feeling worn out. His body had taken quite a beating and he was aching all over. At forty-two, Skeeter was in pretty good shape. Being a gandy dancer took stamina and endurance. But this hobo lifestyle was taking a toll. Palmer on the other hand was looking fresh as a daisy. This was just another day for him. Although he appeared to be at least fifteen years older than Skeeter he was only forty-six. The life of a hobo was not an easy one.

Eventually, Palmer said, "There, to our right." They both stepped off the tracks and entered the woods. A hundred yards or so they reached the jungle.

There were several men all sitting around talking in a low voice. There was a large kettle hanging from an old piece of pipe supported by two branches, one on each side of the fire.

One of the men looked up and spotted Palmer and Skeeter. He smiled as he walked over to greet Palmer. He said, "Hi, Doc, haven't seen you in a long time. Come and have some mulligan and a hundred on a plate."

Skeeter, with a smile on his face, nodded toward Palmer as if to say I got it, I know. Mulligan stew and beans.

"Nice to see you too, Gator," Palmer said to Homer, the man known as Gator, who was from, you got it, Florida, or so he says.

As Palmer greeted Gator, Skeeter nonchalantly looked the jungle over, sizing up its inhabitants. They all appeared to be in need of a shave and a shower. Their clothes were worn and didn't fit quite right. There were fourteen or fifteen people in the jungle, all men. Skeeter also noticed all eyes were looking back at him. They were sizing him up as well.

Palmer reached into his knapsack, fumbled around, and pulled out the two cans of vegetables. He fumbled around in his bag some more and pulled out an old rusty can opener. "Always contribute if you can." He looked at Skeeter with a wink of an eye, "Never know when you will need vegetables."

A light went on in Skeeter's head. He remembered when he asked why Palmer bought two cans of vegetables. Palmer had said, "Never know when you'll need vegetables." Like now.

One of the other men spoke up, "You might even find a piece of meat in the stew." Gator nodded, "That's Jonesy. He trapped a rabbit the other day. Cooked him up, and put him in the stew. Who's the First of May you got with ya?" he asked Palmer nodding toward Skeeter.

In response, Palmer addressed the small crowd, "Listen up, everyone. I would like to introduce my friend Andy Miller. He goes by Slim. He's a construction worker from South Bend."

One of the men said, "In a few years they'll be calling him Fatso!" All the men had a good laugh, then everyone said hi to Skeeter, nodded, or grumbled something. No one believed his name was Andy Miller or that he was a construction worker from South Bend, Indiana. None of them were who they said they were, they all lied about what they did and where they came

from. Most of them used nicknames like Jonesy, Gator, Doc, and Slim. They all had a past.

After the greeting and introduction of Skeeter were over Palmer reached in his bag and pulled outdtwo old tin plates. "Here, Skeeter, I mean Slim. Let's go over and help ourselves to the mulligan and a hundred on a plate." Both stooped close to the fire and ate their meals. Scooping up his last serving of beans, Palmer asked, "Gator, do you know the whereabouts of Dobbs?"

"You mean the carny guy Dobbs?"

"Yeah, I heard he was in the South Bend area."

Another man overheard the conversation and said, "Dobbs is further south. Down around Terre Haute, Sullivan County area. I worked for him for a while. Left about two weeks ago. That's where he should be about now."

Palmer leaned toward Skeeter, "That's a good ways from here. What time you got?"

Skeeter answered, "Eight-thirty."

"We will have to get an early start in the morning. Better hit the sack."

While rolling out his blanket Skeeter looked at Palmer, "No women. Are there women hobos?"

Palmer was somewhat taken back by the question. He smiled and asked, "Getting horny?"

Skeeter was irritated by the implication of the question. He threw his duffel bag on the ground. If you won't give me a straight answer, forget it."

"OK, calm down. Don't get so high and mighty on me. Sure there are women hobos. Not many. As you are finding out, hoboing is a pretty tough life in more ways than one. It is

especially rough on women. Hobo women are called Bo-ette, bims; young hobo women are called heifers. See what I mean? Not much respect. You will see more women in the carnies and they're treated better."

Satisfied with Palmer's explanation, Skeeter said no more and they both laid down and fell fast to sleep.

At sunrise, as Palmer and Skeeter started on their trek south the temperature got warmer. Neither said much as they walked along. Both were thinking of the past. For Palmer, the future wasn't much to think about because it was the same old thing. For Skeeter, a whole new world was opening up.

Chapter 11

Back in Durand, Mary Lou had to apply for welfare. She never really had a job. Never graduated from high school and didn't have any marketable job skills. All she had was a house full of kids, a mortgage, and car payment.

Skeeter's friends and for that matter, the police thought Skeeter did the world a favor by killing Tom Anderson, Bill Barns, and Toby Hicks.

The police went through the formality of an investigation. They sent out state-wide bulletins to all police departments with a picture and description of Skeeter and notified all the railroad companies leading in and out of Michigan. However, the Skeeter Jones case cooled quickly. Anderson, Barns, and Hicks didn't have much of a family life. They didn't have any friends outside of the three of them. It was said their pallbearers might have been hired. There weren't six

friends among the three of them. Few attended their funerals. Some people say Anderson never looked better than when Skeeter blew his head off.

Of course, the mob was not happy with Skeeter. They didn't have the connection in the hobo jungles that they do with the police and in the prison system. But the mob is very patient. They will wait and wait and wait.

Keep running, Skeeter, you are safe as long as you stay moving. The police pursuit is light. The mob will wait, they won't forget, they will wait. Sooner or later the mob believes you will slip up and they will be there.

Chapter 12

It was close to noon. Palmer and Skeeter had a couple of rest stops and made some light chitchat.

"Skeeter, we need to stop for lunch and rest. There is a town just ahead, I will go in and get us something to eat." Skeeter was beginning to get the idea that there are always small towns along a railroad line. He didn't mind at this point. He was famished and ready for a break.

"Are we near where we'll catch a ride?" Skeeter asked, tired of walking.

"No. We will still have a spell to go. Maybe an hour or so. I will need a sawbuck. Do you know how much that is?"

Skeeter looked at him questioningly. "It's ten dollars," Palmer nodded.

Skeeter removed his shoe and gave Palmer a ten-dollar bill. He was catching on to this hobo lingo.

"Stay here, I will be right back."

Skeeter was tired. He noticed some large trees just a few feet off the tracks. He walked over to the trees, tossed his duffel bag down, and sat with his hands on his knees. A slight breeze blowing. *If I had a fishing pole and there was some water I could be fishing just like I used to do on the banks of the Shiawassee.*

A few minutes later Palmer returned. He did not see Skeeter. He looked up and down the track. Still no Skeeter. He started to panic. Did the police happen by and pick him up? Someone whistled. "Over here." He turned and saw Skeeter standing under a tree with a smile on his face. "Over here."

With a loaf of bread, a small jar of peanut butter, another with grape jelly, and two half-pint cartons of chocolate milk, Palmer walked quickly to Skeeter. "Don't scare me like that! I almost had a heart attack!"

As they sat eating their peanut butter jelly sandwiches and drinking the still cool chocolate milk, Skeeter considered his reservations about Palmer's plans. *Let's see, we are going to a place somewhere near Terre Haute, Indiana, on a day and time we are not quite sure of in hopes of meeting a person who we don't know will hire us.*

Skeeter decided to voice his concerns, "Palmer, about this plan of yours..."

Palmer interrupted Skeeter by getting to his feet."Trust me. It is going to be alright. Let's go, we're burning daylight." And on they walked.

By one o'clock Palmer announced, "We're almost there. This station is not as big as South Bend, but still a good size. We will have to be very careful here too."

After they exited the station and added another hundred yards or more in a southerly direction, Palmer said, "Let's get off the tracks and wait for our chariot to arrive."

Moments later he announced, "Here she comes. We didn't get here any too soon. Remember how you got on last time?" As the train passed by, both Palmer and Skeeter ran at top speed. They threw their duffel bags in the boxcar and then swung up and in.

Palmer, with an almost prideful look at Skeeter, told him, "You did better this time, Skeeter. Pretty soon you will be as good as me. We got a long way to go. Sit back and get some shuteye."

They were sound asleep in a matter of seconds. Immediately Skeeter fell into a nightmare about the murders he committed in Durand. His restless slumber was punctuated by twitches and talking in his sleep.

Tap, tap, tap. Palmer was tapping the foot of Skeeter once again. "Come on, it's time to get off." Still sleepy, but thankful the nightmare was over, Skeeter got to his feet. He grabbed his duffel bag and walked slowly to the boxcar door where Palmer was waiting. He was looking at Skeeter, "You look like you've been rode hard and put away wet. You okay?"

Skeeter was standing in the doorway of the boxcar with his eyes closed and hands on his hips feeling the wind blow by. "Yeah. I'm fine. I just have to get used to this hobo routine."

Palmer was looking out the doors. He didn't have time to be sympathetic. Their jump-off location was looming just ahead. In reply, he said, "Remember to follow my lead." Then a moment later Palmer yelled, "Now!" and both men jumped.

Once on the ground they brushed themselves off and righted their belongings.

Palmer walked toward Skeeter, slapped him on the back, and said, "A beautiful three-point landing! A short walk and we should be at the carnival."

"How do you know where the carnival is or even if it's here?"

"I've been here before, just about this time of year. That along with the info we got back at the jungle, I'm pretty sure it's here. The carny will be in the city park. They are usually in parks or any large open piece of land that's close to town. They have a nice park here. Come on, it won't be long now."

Chapter 13

It was a beautiful October afternoon. Palmer and Skeeter strolled down the sidewalk of the town like they didn't have a care in the world. Kings of their own domains. Suddenly Palmer stopped. Pointing to a telephone pole just to the right of the sidewalk, he said, "Look! There is a poster advertising the carny. Let's see what it says." Both men read the poster silently. ***Dobbs' Carnival, October 12-15, Rides! Cotton Candy! Elephant Ears!*** After a moment Palmer said, "Wow! Today is the last day. We better get a move on."

As they entered the carny area Palmer said, "Now to find Dobbs." He looked the area over to find a carny worker. "There are two kinds of people who work at a carnival. Those who are the professional carny workers like you and me, that the carnival hires. Then there are some, mostly food truck operators, who are self-employed and pay the carny owner like Dobbs to set up and do business. Some of these non-carny people follow the carnival

from one site to another, some may follow for just a few setups. The two groups don't usually interact." Palmer paused to look at Skeeter, to see if he was still following along, then went on, "The guys like you and me who run the rides, sideshows, and gyp joints are hobos looking for enough money to buy booze, whiskey, cigarettes. Then they move on."

As Palmer approached a guy at one of the gyp joints, he put his right index finger on the right side of his nose to signal he's a hobo. The huckster at the gyp joint noticed Palmer's signal and signaled back. Palmer offered to shake hands and said, "'Bo." The man shook Palmer's hand and repeated "'Bo."

After affirming their brotherhood, Palmer introduced himself, "I'm Palmer. My friend is Andy. Where's Dobbs? We're looking for a stake."

The huckster pointed to a large faded tent and said, "Over there." The tent was a makeshift mess hall where the carny workers ate their meals.

"Come on, Skeeter, I mean Andy."

Upon entering the tent Palmer saw three men sitting at a table at the end of the mess hall. One was Dobbs. As Palmer and Skeeter approached, the three men stopped talking and looked up in their direction. Palmer shook hands with Dobbs.

"Hello, Mr. Dobbs. Remember me? I worked for you about a year ago." Then turning and nodding toward Skeeter, said, "This is my friend Andy, we're looking for work."

"Oh yeah, I remember you, you're Dr. Palmer." Dobbs gave a sarcastic snort, the two other men at the table gave a little laugh, and he went on. "So you're looking for work." Nodding at

Palmer he said, "I know you're a good worker." Then looking at Skeeter added, "But what about your friend?"

"Andy did a lot of construction work around the South Bend area."

"Can't he talk for himself?" Speaking to Skeeter Dobbs said, "Let me see your hands."

Skeeter stretched out both hands. Dobbs looked at one side then the other. "Yep, you've seen a day's work before. Go with Sam here, he'll show you what to do. I'll get with you later Andy to make out the paperwork."

Palmer, Skeeter, and Sam left the tent. Sam, the head rigger and straw boss of the carny said, "Start knocking down some of the joints first, sideshows, and less popular rides tonight, then get the rest early tomorrow and I mean early. We'll get started at six-thirty. Dobbs, Charlie, and me were talking about getting ready to bug out when you two came in. Charlie was the third man in the mess tent. He's my right-hand man."

The three men were nothing alike. Dobbs was a short, round man, with what might be considered a high forehead, so high it went to the back of his head. His wardrobe was always the same white short sleeve shirt, black bow tie, khaki trousers held up by both suspenders and belt. He was very streetwise. He knew most of the carny workers were on the run from something. Sam was tall and slim and always had a five o'clock shadow. He was the head rigger in charge of the setup and tear down of the carnival. He was also responsible for making sure the old worn-out equipment ran. He was not overly bright, maybe had an IQ of 85. His right-hand man, Charlie, was forever loyal to both Sam and Dobbs, but not as bright as Sam. He was

medium built, always in need of a shave worse than Sam. He had a few teeth missing in the front, maybe a few in the back, but always had a smile.

While chewing his Redman Tobacco, Sam pointed and said, “Start with this one.” It was a tent that housed a gyp joint.” He spit and resumed speaking to Palmer, “You say you done this before?”

“Oh yeah. A lot of times.”

“OK, you and your buddy take it down. When you're done come and get me. I’ll be over there,” pointing to one of the rides with a greasy finger. “Shouldn’t take you guys much more than an hour to get this job done.”

After Sam left, Skeeter asked Palmer, “What kind of paperwork does Dobbs want me to fill out? What type of information do I need to lie about now?” Skeeter was getting nervous about questions like *What’s your address? Have you ever been arrested or convicted of a felony? What’s your full name?* And how about: *Have you blown anyone's head off lately?*

Palmer understood completely, “All he wants you to do is fill out an employment application. Remember to lie to every question. Name? Andrew Miller. Address? Put down any street name and number that comes to you in South Bend, Indiana. What kind of work do you do? Construction worker. Who did you work for? Make up any name. Have you ever been arrested? No. Social Security number? Make one up. He will never turn it into the government. Dobbs just wants to cover his butt. He will put the application in his file cabinet and never look at it again. If the police ever come asking about you all he needs to say is

'here is all the information I have on him'. Dobbs knows the background of the people that work for him." This eased Skeeter's very cramped mind.

After Palmer and Skeeter finished tearing down the tent and wrapping it up they walked over to Sam who was dismantling the Tilt-A-Whirl.

Palmer was feeling proud of the job he and Skeeter did and said with some pride, "We're done!"

Wiping his hands on a rag, Sam stepped down from the scaffolding and said, "Let's have a look." They walked the short distance back to the site where the gyp joint tent was laying. Sam checked out their work. "Good job, looks like everything's fine."

"Andy, the boss wants to see you," Sam said, nodding to a red moving van. "He's over there in that red van. "Sam hooked his thumb in another direction, "Palmer, come on, we'll start on some other gyp joints." Palmer and Sam headed off.

Skeeter, still nervous about filling out the employment application, started off in the opposite direction to meet with Dobbs. He kept thinking about what Palmer said. Lie, lie about everything. When Skeeter arrived he knocked on the door of the eighteen feet long cargo van. A voice, loud and gruff from inside bellowed, "Come in!"

Skeeter opened the door and stepped inside. Much to his surprise, the interior of the van was converted into a small office. Dobbs was sitting on a wooden office chair with rollers behind a metal desk which was virtually empty except for a green desk lamp. The walls and ceiling were wood-paneled with an inexpensive vinyl floor. In front of Dobbs' desk were two chairs,

and off to one side was a small couch none of which matched, along with a three drawer filing cabinet and a small safe.

Dobbs looked up and with a wave toward one of the chairs, said, “Sit down, have a seat, Andy.” Skeeter sat on the edge of the chair with his knee bouncing in perpetual motion. Dobbs handed a single sheet of paper to him. “Fill out this employment application. Not much to it. It's just for my records.” Dobbs knew Skeeter was going to lie about everything. “You can fill it out right here. It won’t take you long.” Skeeter took the application and started filling it out. Dobbs added, “If you have any questions, just ask.”

Sure enough, the application was just like Palmer said. Name and address and so on. Remember: lie, lie, lie.

A few minutes later Skeeter completed the application and handed it back to Dobbs. He lied on every question. This lying business was new to Skeeter. He might have been a lot of things, heavy drinker, barroom brawler, but what he wasn’t was a liar. One of the things Skeeter disliked in a person was dishonesty, lying, cheating, stealing. Skeeter didn’t do those things. Now, he might take a shotgun and blow your head off, but wouldn't lie or cheat you in any way.

Dobbs scanned the application looking as if he cared about the information. He dropped the application on his desk and asked, “Got any questions?”

“Not really.” Skeeter had lots of questions but was pretty sure the less he said, the better off he was. He didn’t want to do or say anything that he would regret later.

Dobbs smiled and went on, “Here's what your employment package is: Three hots and a cot. The meals are in

the mess tent. Breakfast is usually at seven, but tomorrow it's at six because of the teardown. We want to get an early start. Lunch is at noon, dinner at five. It's on a first-come-first-served basis. He who tarries eats last, or something like that. Your pay is a share of the profits. I have a somewhat complex breakdown as to how much each person gets. It is based on how long you've been with me and what you do." What Dobbs really meant is *You get paid whatever I want to pay you.* "One of the semi-trailers is used as the bunkhouse. It has lights and heat."

What he failed to mention was the "lights" was one sixty watt light bulb hanging in the center of the forty-eight-foot windowless trailer, and the "heat" he referred to was a small kerosene stove located at the back end near the doors so, hopefully, there is enough ventilation you won't die. Bunk beds lined the walls to accommodate up to twenty-eight transient workers. "I'll have you bunk with Palmer." Dobbs gave the bunkhouse a cursory description, and Skeeter could only imagine why. He had a feeling this would not be the Holiday Inn.

"Any questions?" Dobbs paused knowing there wouldn't be any. "If not, find Sam and Palmer. They're probably tearing down some of the kiddie rides."

Skeeter stood, shook hands with Dobbs, and said, "Thanks for the job." He turned and left Dobbs' little office and started looking for Sam and Palmer. Skeeter thought *What a bright sunny day.* With a slight breeze coming from the food carts he could smell cotton candy and popcorn just as he did when he was at the Shiawassee County Fair back at McCurdy Park in Corunna, Michigan.

After a few minutes, he found Palmer and Sam. He gave Palmer a wink and a nod as if to say everything is OK and started right in helping them without saying a word.

After getting the tent knockdown completed, Skeeter said to Sam, "Dobbs said that you will show Palmer and me where to bunk."

"Oh, you mean Mr. Dobbs!" Sam said setting Skeeter straight on the proper protocol. "We'll finish working. Have some chow. Then I'll show you."

A couple of hours later Sam waved his hand in the direction of Palmer and Skeeter and said, "Chow time." He started walking toward the mess tent.

Once the three of them got to the mess hall a line had already started to form. The meal was served cafeteria-style. They picked up a tray, plate, bowl, silverware and moved down the line. The hash slingers were some of the women hobos who put the food on the plate. This day the cooks were serving up scumgullion, which was the same as mulligan stew, hundred-on-a-plate, a slice of bread with no butter, and black coffee, no sugar. The stew and beans weren't much better than Skeeter had in the jungle. The coffee was worse.

Palmer and Skeeter sat down at one of the long tables and started to eat. A man sitting next to Skeeter pointed at his food and said, "If you think this is bad, wait for breakfast."

After dinner, Palmer and Skeeter took a long walk around the park making small talk. Palmer let Skeeter in on the dos and don'ts of carny life. Do what you're told, don't trust anyone, and lie about everything. Skeeter, still not knowing anything about his new world, unloaded a barrage of questions

on Palmer, "Where do we go from here? How long do we stay with the carny? Am I safe from the police being so out in the open?"

Palmer, being ever so patient with Skeeter calmly answered, "We will stay with the carny until the end of the season, about late November to early December depending on Dobbs' bookings. Dobbs, along with most of the smaller carnies and circuses, winters in Florida near a town called Gibsonton. He pays a fee to park the trucks and equipment until spring. From then until spring you're on your own. Some workers hang around the parked equipment. They stay in the semi-trailers just like they did when they were on the road. The only difference is there isn't any heat or light. They pick up odd jobs, some panhandle, and others ride the rails. The smart ones stay south in the winter, the snowball eaters travel north. As far as the law is concerned there's no safer place outside of your mother's womb than a carny or circus. Carnivals travel far from where hobos commit their crimes so most of the time nobody has heard of what they've done and over time their indiscretions and crimes fade away."

Palmer noticed Skeeter didn't look any more relaxed at these words, so he went on, "I really doubt if the law is pursuing you that much right now. The guys you killed were not that well-loved. Not by the police anyway. The mob might still be after you, but remember, they don't have the connections in the jungle and carnies that they have with the police. They will wait until the law gets you, then they will have you."

At this Skeeter's face drained of color, so Palmer was quick to add with a smile and squeeze to the shoulder, "Stay on

the rails, work the carnies. You will be alright." Skeeter looked up feeling a bit safer.

Palmer noticed the sun getting low and said, "Let's get back to the bunkhouse before it gets too late. Some of the guys go to sleep early and they don't like being woke up."

"I keep hearing about the men doing this and doing that, but what about the women? Where do they bunk?"

"Ah, you noticed the women? There are always a few around. The women usually work in the mess tent helping prepare food, sling hash, doing dishes. A few run the gyp joints and the kiddie rides. It seems parents trust women around their kids more than men. They don't get paid as much, just like in the real world. Remember I told you, in the jungle the men refer to the older women as 'beefers' and the younger ones as 'heifers'. To answer your question, no, the women don't sleep in the same trailer with the men, they have one of the smaller trailers of their own. It has been known that some men occasionally make a midnight run to the women's trailer and for a dollar or two they will get their pleasure. I would recommend you stay away. You can smell most of them before you can see them. The more attractive ones have most of their teeth and they shower maybe once a week if there are showers at the parks. They wear their clothes just like we do, until they fall off. Besides all that you just might get a little more than you ask for."

Neither Palmer nor Skeeter made the midnight runs. They both valued money too much. Skeeter even quit smoking to save money.

As they were about to enter the bunkhouse Palmer, speaking in a low voice said, "Let's go in quietly. Go as far to the

front of the trailer as possible, that way we can keep a good eye on the rest of the other guys. Sleep with one eye open and keep your pistol close by. Remember some of these guys will cut your throat for fifty cents."

When Palmer opened the door he could see through the dimly lit trailer that there was a spot at the very front. The trailer was lined on both sides with bunk beds. Not many people had arrived yet. They both moved forward, found their bunks, got settled, and tried to get some sleep.

Sometime in the night among the snoring, farting, coughing, and hacking of the twenty-seven other souls, Skeeter fell asleep.

All of a sudden Skeeter felt Palmer nudging at his elbow. Palmer leaned over and whispered in his ear, "Look."

Skeeter, only half awake, had an eerie feeling that someone was looking at him. After his eyes adjusted to the darkness, he looked up to see a man crawling toward him.

Very slowly he placed his hand on the pistol that he put inside his blanket. Just as the man reached Skeeter's foot, in one smooth motion Skeeter sat up and drew out his pistol. He pointed it at the man and said, "Don't." Without a word, the man crawled backward toward his bed.

The rest of the night there was normal activity in the bunkhouse with a couple of the men leaving very stealthily and then returning with smiles on their faces, a twinkle in their eyes, and two dollars poorer.

As the sun was rising in the east on a crisp October morning, Sam was beating on the door shouting, "It's six A.M.! Time for you bums to get off and on. Better get it while it's hot."

Everyone scrambled to get out the door and down to the mess tent for that something-similar-to-oatmeal, a slice of bread, no butter, and black coffee, no sugar.

While Palmer and Skeeter were eating, Sam walked over to them, bent over, and said in a low voice, "I heard what happened last night with the gun. I don't want any trouble."

Skeeter assured him, "You will have no trouble from me."

From then on Palmer and Skeeter never had any problems with anyone.

Every day was like the one before. Rise early in the morning, eat the same breakfast in the mess tent: oatmeal, bread, no butter, coffee black, no sugar. Lunch was some kind of sandwich, usually peanut butter. On good days when Dobbs had extra money, which wasn't very often, and was in a good mood, which wasn't often, you might get jelly, black coffee, and still no sugar. Workers never left their work site for lunch. Instead, they would have to eat between loading people on and off the rides or at a slow time at the gyp joints. Dinners were eaten in the mess tent, but they had staggered times so people could leave their job site. You could go eat if someone would relieve you. Dinners were mulligan stew and hundred-on-a-plate, bread, you got it, no butter, coffee black, no sugar.

The workweek was seven days. The average workday was from eleven A.M. until at least ten P.M. Pay was every two or three or four weeks. Whatever Dobbs said. Dobbs paid Sam and Charlie more since Sam was the straw boss and Charlie was Sam's right-hand man. Everyone else was paid whatever Dobbs wanted. The pay was never the same. Sometimes you would get

forty dollars, sometimes fifty, sometimes thirty. Your pay was three hots and a cot and maybe a dollar an hour. No one complained, at least not to Dobbs. He said it was based on profits. Every payday he would say, "Hard times, hard times, we are falling on hard times." In all fairness to Dobbs, the carny business is a very tough business to be in.

Chapter 14

Days turned into weeks. They moved from one small town to another. Setup, tear down. Work the rides, work gyp joints. Ten to twelve hours a day every day.

Dobbs kept a good eye on all of his workers. He never really trusted any of them, not even Sam and Charlie who had been with him for some time. He noticed that Skeeter was a good worker. He always started on time and seemed to have a smile.

One morning during breakfast Dobbs motioned for Skeeter to come to the table where he, Sam, and Charlie were eating. "I have been noticing you, Andy, you do good work. I would like to move you to a better job. It will be more pay." Not really, Dobbs will pay him what Dobbs wants to pay. "Not everybody can do this job."

Skeeter was thrilled at the prospect of earning more money, "Wow! Better job, more pay. What is it?"

Dobbs leaned back in his chair and put his thumbs under his suspenders. "We'll need to train you some. I think you can handle it. I would like to move you from rigger to huckster. With your gift to gab, you will do quite well." Most of Skeeter's life he had been quick with a smile, had a pleasant personality, and quick with a joke.

"Thanks, Boss, I will do my best."

Skeeter was happy and somewhat proud. He got a promotion. In all areas of work, there is a pecking order, one job is better than the other. Skeeter's promotion from rides to huckster would have the others looking at Skeeter and saying "Wow! From ride jockey to huckster in such a short time, he must have been sucking up to Dobbs." Even in a carnival world, it seems there are people jealous of others' jobs.

In a few days, you could see Skeeter standing in front of his game with a big smile on his face with a short thin cane in his hand pointing to the several prizes that someone could win. Dressed with a black derby hat, his light brown hair sticking out in the front, black bow tie, red and white striped shirt, Skeeter could be heard hawking, "Step right up! Take your chance! Win your honey a cupie doll! For just ten cents, one thin dime, one-tenth of a dollar, you can be a hero!"

Skeeter was becoming quite the man about camp. Palmer was proud of him. Even the beefers and heifers started coming around with big toothless smiles and offered Skeeter a freebie every once in a while.

Chapter 15

It was six-thirty on a chilly early December morning in southeast Florida. This was the last week of carny season for the Dobbs gang. Everyone was glad and sad at the same time. On the last day, Dobbs gave everyone a little bonus.

Outside the bunk trailer came the morning banging on the door to get up. “Get it while it’s hot! Come on, we're burning daylight.” It was the human alarm clock, Sam. Everybody scrambled around to be first in line for breakfast. The food may not be that good, but it was hot and the morning was cool.

“Come on, old buddy!” Skeeter was tapping on the bottom of Palmer’s foot. “We need to get going before these vultures eat it all up.” In the past, it was Palmer getting up first and tapping Skeeter on the foot to wake him up. Lately, it has been the other way around.

Skeeter had noticed that Palmer was not himself lately. He wasn't moving as fast, and he seemed to have a little nagging cough. When Skeeter would ask Palmer how he was feeling he would say, "I'm OK, just getting older. Who is the doctor here, you or me?"

Skeeter persisted, "Come on, get up!" He started tapping Palmer on the bottom of his foot again. "Come on, old man, let's go."

Nothing. Skeeter knelt beside Palmer and started shaking him by his shoulders. "Come on, get up." Skeeter looked into the eyes of his old friend, they were open and staring straight forward. Skeeter's heart started beating fast. With a trembling hand, Skeeter placed his fingers on his friend's neck to get a pulse. Nothing. Palmer was dead. Skeeter slumped down and picked up the best friend and partner he ever had and began to weep. Whispering in Palmer's ear, Skeeter said, "I love you, Dr. C. William Palmer, M. D."

In the coming days, Skeeter would view the death of Palmer as more profound in light of all the other losses in his life - his wife, children, job, freedom, identity. Yes, they were losses that would never be found. However, Skeeter came to depend on Palmer the way a child would a father, and now he was gone.

Skeeter laid Palmer on his bunk, closed his eyes, and placed a dirty old blanket over him. He hadn't felt this kind of loss since the death of his son. The bunkhouse was empty except for Skeeter and Palmer. Everyone was at the mess tent eating breakfast. Skeeter, with tears in his eyes, started walking slowly toward the mess tent with his head hung down and feeling sick to his stomach. The cool morning air started to help clear his head

and calm him down. Once inside the tent, Skeeter walked to Dobbs. Dobbs could tell by the look on Skeeter's face something was wrong.

"Good morning, Andy, what's up?"

With his eyes full of tears and in a slow gravelly voice Skeeter said, "Palmer's dead." Sitting near Dobbs, both Sam and Charlie heard what Skeeter said. All three looked shocked. "Where is he?"

"Back at the bunkhouse. I covered him up with a blanket."

Dobbs was shocked. He had no idea Palmer was that sick. Dobbs knew this was going to cause quite a stir around the camp. Carny workers are superstitious about death in the camp. They believe death comes in threes. Thoughts were whirling around in Dobbs' head. What to do next? Notify the police. Keep the camp calm. He still had to take care of business and get ready for the winter.

After quickly processing the situation, Dobbs gave the orders, "Sam, you come with me and Andy. Charlie, you stay here to see that things get started for the day. Anyone asks where we are, tell them we're making arrangements for the winter."

As they left for the bunkhouse, Dobbs asked Skeeter, "What do you think happened, Andy?"

"I don't know. He hasn't been looking well. He had a cough. I don't know, maybe just old age."

When they got to the bunkhouse Dobbs opened the door and all three men walked to the front of the trailer. Palmer's poor old, worn-out body was just a lump under a dirty blanket. Dobbs bent down over Palmer's body and pulled back the blanket. He

reached down and put his fingers to the side of Palmer's neck to feel for a pulse, hoping that maybe Skeeter was wrong, that Palmer was just deep in sleep. With his fingers still on his neck, Dobbs looked at Skeeter and said in a sympathetic voice, "He's dead alright."

Standing next to Skeeter, Sam said, "He took the westbound."

Skeeter didn't understand. "What do you mean 'he took the westbound'?"

"That's what hobos say when someone dies."

Dobbs, still kneeling at the side of Palmer, placed the blanket back over Palmer. "Well, I'll call the local police."

The police. Skeeter was stunned, his face turned white, his heart beat fast again. Thoughts whipped through his mind, *Will the police way down here in Florida know that I killed Anderson, Barns, and Hicks? Will they know there is a nationwide search for me? Pull it together, Skeeter! Palmer always said no one will miss the three of them. They had no family, only the mob. Everything is going to be OK. Calm down, roll with the punches thrown at you.*

As Dobbs stood he said, "They will call a local funeral home to come get him. They may or may not call the coroner's office. Most of the time people in the real world don't much care what happens to us when we are alive, let alone when we're dead. It's a real problem."

Skeeter was still looking at his old friend. "Who's going to pay for the funeral?"

Dobbs understood where Skeeter was coming from. "It all comes down to money. If you don't have any and you die,

you become a problem. He will probably have a pauper's funeral." Dobbs let that sink in then continued, "You know, Andy, someone will need to be in charge of Palmer's estate, such as it is."

"What does that mean?"

"You're the only resemblance of a family Palmer's got. The funeral director will ask you a few questions about the burial. The police will ask you questions about what happened prior to Palmer's death. There won't be many questions either way. They will just want to get it over with." Dobbs turned to Sam, "You stay here with Andy. I'll call the police. Don't let anyone in the trailer. Just tell them to go to work."

A few minutes later Dobbs returned to the bunkhouse. "Well, I called the police. They should be here shortly. They said they would notify the funeral home. There is only one funeral home in town called the Leonard Smalley Funeral Home. Smalley also happens to be the Assistant County Coroner. That makes everything much easier."

Just about the time it took for Dobbs to walk from his office and explain what was about to happen, the police showed up.

Getting out of his car and walking toward the bunkhouse was not just a policeman but the chief of police himself, Robert Moore. Chief Moore was not only the chief of police, he was also the head of emergency services, which included fire, police, and ambulance. Chief Moore wanted to make sure the handling of the death of this vagrant was handled quickly and smoothly. Nothing in the papers. Get the dead guy to the funeral home and get him buried just as if nothing happened.

Dobbs greeted the chief at the door to the bunkhouse. "Come in, Officer.

Moore shook hands with Dobbs. "I am Chief Moore." The chief made it clear from the get-go he was not just a policeman but Chief of Police.

"I'm Dobbs, owner of this Carnival." Dobbs led the chief to the front of the trailer where Skeeter and Sam were standing next to the body of Palmer. "Chief, I would like you to meet Sam, my straw boss, and this gentleman," he pointed to Skeeter, "is Andy Miller. Andy works for me and was a close friend of the deceased." Dobbs made sure not to call Chief Moore "officer" but "Chief" giving him due respect.

The chief was a very average-looking man who appeared to be in his fifties. After spending a few years with the county police he joined the local police as a patrolman and worked his way through the ranks to Chief of Police.

Moore reached into his pocket and pulled out a pencil and a small pad of paper. "Who can tell me about the deceased?"

Dobbs pointed toward Skeeter. "He probably knows the most. They were very close."

Chief Moore, with pencil and paper in hand, turned to Skeeter, "Ok, Mr. Miller, tell me what you know."

With teary eyes and a trembling voice, Skeeter appeared to be very sad and grieving, however, he was more scared than anything. With Chief Moore standing two feet away asking all kinds of questions, Skeeter wondered if he could lie his way out of this one. "His name is Palmer. C. William Palmer. Everybody called him Palmer. We've been good friends for a while. I don't know much about his family. I don't think he has any."

"Where did you say you two are from?"

"South Bend."

South Bend, Indiana I take it. Gets really cold up there this time of year."

"Yeah. South Bend, Indiana. Yeah, real cold."

Dobbs gave a questioning look at Skeeter. Dobbs knew that Palmer was from a small town outside Pittsburgh. That is what Palmer put on his employment application.

Skeeter noticed Dobbs' questioning look.

"What can you tell me, Mr. -," The chief paused, struggling to recall Skeeter's last name.

"Just call me Skeeter, I mean Andy, Andy Miller." Skeeter was very nervous. He just made two critical mistakes. He couldn't think straight. He was unable to keep up with all the names he had and all the lies that he had told.

The chief didn't appear to have picked up on Skeeter's slip of the tongue or maybe he just didn't want to. All he was thinking was *Let's get this mess over with.*

Skeeter told the chief about Palmer not looking well and his bad cough.

Chief Moore was scribbling on his pad of paper. "Probably pneumonia."

Standing at the far end of the trailer was a man tapping on the open door. "Can we come in?" It was Leonard Smalley of Smalley Funeral Home. With him was his employee and want-to-be mortician, Elroy, but everyone in town called him Roy.

The chief motioned for the two to come to the front of the trailer.

Smalley was smoking a large cigar. He appeared to be in his mid-sixties. He stood about five feet ten and weighed about two hundred and fifty pounds. He was dressed in a black suit and black bowtie. Roy was a tall young man, six feet tall, and weighed one-eighty. Roy did all the heavy lifting for Smalley.

"Here he is," Moore said, pointing to Palmer. Once Smalley and Roy reached the front of the bunkhouse, the chief greeted and introduced them to Skeeter, Dobbs, and Sam.

Smalley stooped down the best he could and tried to get a pulse from Palmer. He removed a small flashlight from his coat pocket, lifted each of Palmer's eyelids, and waved the light across each eye. Smalley looked up at his assistant and told him to take note, "Roy, I pronounce Mr. Palmer deceased at," Smalley looked at his watch, "eight oh five A.M. on this day. You fill in the blanks, Roy."

Red-faced and out of breath, his two hundred fifty pounds going in different directions, Smalley struggled to get to his feet. "Tell me what preceded Mr. Palmer's death, Mr. Ah - " Smalley had forgotten Skeeter's name.

"Andy, Andy Miller." At this point, Skeeter was wondering what his own name was as well. He repeated how Palmer was acting, his coughing.

Chief Moore asked, "What do you think, Leonard? Pneumonia?"

"Probably. We will see." Addressing his assistant he said, "Roy, get the gurney and bring it in here. We will take Mr. Palmer to the funeral home." Then addressing Skeeter went on, "Andy, you will need to come with us and fill out the paperwork."

Skeeter was thinking *Not more paperwork, more lies...* but he said, "I don't have a ride." There was no room for Skeeter to ride in the hearse with Smalley and his two hundred fifty plus pounds and Roy and for sure no room in the back with Palmer. Chief Moore said, "I'll give you a ride. It is only a few blocks from here."

Smalley finally caught his breath and said, "I will have Roy bring you back."

Roy and Sam put Palmer into a body bag, onto the gurney, then out the trailer door into the hearse that doubled as an ambulance.

Chapter 16

Not only did Smalley own the funeral home in town, but he also ran the ambulance service. When the hearse-ambulance, known as the Gray Ghost was not being used as a hearse it was an ambulance. When used as a hearse the Gray Ghost was clad with little purple curtains on the side and rear windows. On the side windows were silver letters about two inches high spelling out *Leonard Smalley Funeral Home*. It pays to advertise. When used as an ambulance, down came the pretty purple curtains, off came the *Leonard Smalley Funeral Home* sign, and placed on top of the Gray Ghost was a red flashing light. When used, the Gray Ghost's siren could sound out with the best of them.

It's true that twenty percent of the people do eighty percent of the work and in a small town like Gibsonton, it's no different. The town of Gibsonton, and Smalley's position in it, is similar to small towns all over America that are run and governed by people who wear many hats. The hardware, gas

station, and insurance owners may all be volunteer firefighters, city council members, and volunteer ambulance attendants.

Leonard Smalley wore several important hats. When the townspeople needed an ambulance the call went to the emergency services dispatcher which was, you got it, located at Smalley Funeral Home. They dispatched for ambulance, fire, and police. Smalley even blew the fire siren at the fire hall every day at noon. This was done to make sure it was working. The noonday siren also let everyone in town and for a mile away know that it was twelve o'clock. You know, time for lunch.

The chief and Skeeter got into the police car and followed the hearse into town. Arriving at the funeral home the chief pulled up to a side door which was the entrance to the funeral home's office. Smalley, Roy, and Palmer went to the back of the funeral home to unload Palmer where they would then take him to the embalming room to prepare Palmer's body.

"Go inside, Andy, they will take good care of you and your friend." Skeeter got out of the police car, walked up a few steps, and entered the funeral home office. He was immediately greeted by a short plump pleasant-looking woman in her late fifties.

She said, "Hello, I'm Martha, Leonard's wife. Come this way to the office and we will get started with the paperwork. Leonard and I will try to answer any questions you might have." Once in the office, Martha took a seat behind a desk, she smiled and pointed to a chair, "Have a seat, Mr. -."

"Miller, but please just call me Andy."

"Andy it is. We like to be as informal as we can. Leonard and I know most of the people in town on a personal basis."

"It must be hard to, I mean difficult to, I mean." His tongue was getting all tied up. "You know what I mean?"

"No. It isn't a problem for Leonard and me to take care of people we know. We feel we perform a needed service to the deceased and their families. We do everything we can in a very loving and caring manner. We will do the same for you. Here, Andy, are the forms you need to fill out. Take your time. Would you like a cup of coffee or a soda? I make a pretty good cup of coffee."

"Thanks, yes. Coffee, please."

"I will bring you some cream and sugar so you can fix it the way you like."

Skeeter was thinking *Cream and sugar! When was the last time I had cream and sugar for my coffee?*

Skeeter started to read the forms Martha had given him. Name of the deceased, date of birth, address, and on and on. *Remember what Palmer said: lie, lie, lie. So many lies told, so many lies to tell, how can I keep track of them all?* With his leg jiggling, he labored to answer each question.

Martha returned with the coffee. "Here you go, Andy, fresh hot brewed coffee. I brought you a couple of brownies I baked this morning. I thought you might like them while you're filling out all those forms. Take your time. When you finish," she pointed to a buzzer on the desk, "just push this button, it rings in the next room. It will let me know when you're done. I

will be doing paperwork of my own." She chuckled and walked away.

Skeeter sat alone in the office with his hot fresh brewed coffee, cream, sugar, and brownies. *How thoughtful of Martha! She isn't trying to impress anyone, least of all me because she knows where Palmer and I come from.* Martha treated Skeeter just like anyone else, maybe better. *She and her husband aren't going to make any profit from this funeral. Maybe she is just a nice person. Haven't bumped into many of those lately.*

Skeeter finished the forms and buzzed Martha. She returned and sat at her desk. "OK, let me have those forms." She looked at them and said, "Everything looks good." She picked up the phone and dialed, "Leonard, you can come here now? Andy is done filling out the forms."

A moment later, Leonard entered the office. He walked over to Andy without sitting down and in a business-like tone addressed the matter at hand, "I understand you are anxious to know what is going to happen. Let me explain as much as I can, and if you have any questions when I finish, I will do my best to answer them." Skeeter sat with both hands on his legs waiting patiently for Leonard to get started.

"First, we will prepare Mr. Palmer, embalm him, and place him in a casket, which the county will pay for." Skeeter's face went blank and he was feeling a little nauseous. He didn't feel like he was even present. He didn't hear what Smalley was saying. *Embalm Palmer. Put him in a casket. Palmer is really dead.*

Smalley saw the look on Skeeter's face and stopped his explanation, "Are you alright?"

Taking a deep breath Skeeter answered, "Yeah, I'm OK." He snapped out of his momentary daze. "Yes, I'm OK," he repeated.

Smalley continued, "You or anyone else that would choose to see Mr. Palmer can visit him in our viewing room at twelve o'clock tomorrow. After the viewing, we will transport Mr. Palmer to the county cemetery where he will be buried in the section for the indigent."

As executor, Skeeter realized that he might be responsible for the expenses of this funeral. He also knew he had absolutely no money to cover the costs. "Mr. Smalley, I don't have the funds to cover this."

Smalley assured Skeeter, "Although the amount paid by most government-funded funerals barely covers the embalming, all costs will be paid by the county and state. Let me be completely honest with you. We will provide a very modest funeral. It will consist of a cardboard casket, vault, the opening and closing of the grave. He will have his own gravesite rather than a common burial site that is typical of many pauper burials."

Skeeter looked at the floor and thought of poor Palmer. At one time in his life, he was a doctor, husband, and father. His family was so proud of him. He will be buried as a pauper, a hobo. No one will know or care except Skeeter. "Will he have a marker of any kind?"

Leonard spoke up quickly, "No. I am afraid not."

Skeeter calculated in his mind the money that he and Palmer had saved. Maybe two hundred or so. "How much would a cheap one, I mean an inexpensive one be?"

Leonard wanted to just get this job over. It wouldn't result in any money in his pocket. He blew a puff of smoke from the large cigar that he was smoking. He recited a rough estimate, "I don't know, maybe a thousand dollars or more."

"Wow! I didn't know they cost that much. I only got a hundred or so."

Martha interrupted, "Leonard, you might be able to use a bronze marker with Mr. Palmer's name, date of birth, and date of death on it. That wouldn't be much, would it? Maybe a hundred or so."

Leonard looked at his wife. Martha's usual smile was gone and in its place was a look of pleading.

Leonard knew even a bronze marker would be more than a hundred dollars. "I guess we could."

Skeeter sat up straight realizing that just maybe Palmer's grave would not go unmarked. "What is a bronze marker like?"

"Here I'll show you." Martha opened a drawer to the desk and pulled out a book that had several different headstones. She turned to the page of a flat bronze marker. "See," she said, pointing to a picture, "they're quite nice and durable. I think this one would be very nice for your friend. The cost would be one hundred dollars." Martha looked to her husband, her face begging him to agree, "Isn't that right, Leonard?"

She pulled back the book so Skeeter couldn't see the price of the marker that was plainly marked **RETAIL: $200, WHOLESALE $100.**

Leonard realized what Martha was up to. "Yes, that's correct, Martha."

She turned back to Skeeter. “The people at the cemetery will pour a cement base and bolt the marker to it. The cost of the base is included in the one hundred dollars, isn't it Leonard?” Again, giving Leonard the look.

“Yes, Martha. Included in the one hundred dollars.”

Martha continued, “Some military people use this same kind of marker, don’t they, Leonard?

“Yes, they do, Martha.”

Skeeter interjected, “Palmer’s name. Could it read ‘Dr. C. William Palmer’?

Martha said matter of factly, “I don’t see why not. Whatever you think best, Andy.”

“Will there be a preacher at the funeral?”

Leonard knows that anything beyond the typical pauper’s funeral will come out of his pocket. “Normally there....”

Martha quickly responded before her husband could say another word, “Yes, one can be arranged. Right, Leonard?” Leonard did not say a word, he just nodded his head as if to say “Yes, Martha.”

Skeeter figured he still had some money left. “How much would he charge?”

Martha jumped in with a price, “Maybe ten dollars,” knowing that it would be more like twenty.

Leonard just nodded his head.

“Let’s see,” Skeeter clumsily pulled his very worn billfold from his pocket. “One hundred dollars for the bronze marker, ten for the preacher. Would twenty dollars buy some flowers for Palmer?”

“Absolutely!”

Leonard turned his head and rolled his eyes as if to say this is going to cost me a bundle.

"Here is a hundred and fifty dollars. That should cover it."

Leonard was no pushover. He could be a tough man to live with. He pinched every penny. What Leonard also knew was Martha had a warm heart. She saw in Skeeter a person who wanted to do the right thing for his friend; he just didn't have enough money.

Leonard looked whipped from the financial beating that Martha had given him. With a sigh, he said, "We will see you tomorrow at noon. Roy will pick you and a couple of your friends up if they want to come. Martha, would you get a hold of Roy? Have him bring the car around for Andy."

Skeeter got to his feet and shook hands with Leonard. Martha came from behind the desk and gave Skeeter a hug, "See you tomorrow, Andy."

Chapter 17

As Skeeter left the funeral home, Roy was waiting outside to give Skeeter a ride back to the carnival. Neither Skeeter nor Roy said a word until they arrived at the carnival. Skeeter opened the door, got out, looked back at Roy, and said, "Thanks."

Roy nodded.

Skeeter looked around not knowing where to go. He just started walking with his head down, hands in his pockets, not going in any particular direction with all of his thoughts on Palmer, the funeral, and the police. Skeeter looked up and found himself at the door of Dobbs' office. He knocked on the door.

Dobbs, from inside the trailer shouted out in his normally gruff voice, "Come in!"

Skeeter opened the door and walked in.

Dobbs, in a much softer voice, said, “Sit down, Andy. How did it go at the funeral home?”

“Quite well. Mr. and Mrs. Smalley are very nice. I filled out all the paperwork.” Skeeter explained all the funeral arrangements he’d discussed with the Smalleys. Then he added, “The viewing for Palmer will be tomorrow at noon. They said anyone can come that wants to. I thought maybe you might want to go. If you do, can I get a ride?”

Dobbs, not looking at Skeeter, reverted to his business mode and said, “Well, we will be finishing our last day here tomorrow, for that matter the last day of the season. Got a lot of work to do.” Dobbs then looked into Skeeter's eyes. “Sure, I’ll go, maybe Sam, too if that’s all right.”

Skeeter’s eyes start to tear up. “That's great. Do you think I could take the time to wash out my clothes? I would like to look as good as I can for Palmer.”

“Take all the time you want, Andy. Get some rest. You don’t have to do any more work. Let me see if I can get one of the women to wash your clothes. Leave the clothes you want washed at the door of the bunkhouse and someone will pick them up.”

Skeeter got to his feet, shook hands with Dobbs, and said, “Thanks. I guess I will try and get some sleep.” He left Dobbs’ office and went back to the bunkhouse and lay down on his bunk. As he did so, he grabbed the blanket he’d covered Palmer’s body with, and clutched it to himself as he closed his eyes hoping for sleep, “Good night, Palmer.” Skeeter drifted off into a collage of dreams. Mary Lou, the kids, shooting pool at

the 602, working on the rails, shooting Anderson. One after the other, waking up in a cold sweat. Back to sleep. More dreams.

After Skeeter left his office to get some rest, Dobbs went to the mess tent where they were preparing lunch. Some of the women who work there also do washing and ironing for the other workers to make an extra dollar or two.

Dobbs found a toothless woman named Pearl and explained the extraordinary funeral arrangements Skeeter made with Smalley. "He even has arranged to have a burial marker and flowers! I would like to do something nice for Andy. Would you wash and iron Andy's clothes? I'll pay to have it done."

Pearl answered with a smile, "I'll do it, I'll do it for nothing. I'll do it for Andy."

"Go to the door of the bunkhouse and his clothes will be there. By the way, thanks." She nodded.

And almost instantly the news about what Skeeter had arranged for Palmer's funeral spread throughout the workers.

Lunchtime came and went. The workers ate their lunches and returned to work. It was now around five forty-five p.m. Dobbs opened the bunkhouse door and saw Andy's laundry lying on the floor. Pearl had delivered them freshly washed, ironed, neatly folded, and placed them exactly where Dobbs said.

Looking down the dimly lit bunkhouse trailer, Dobbs could see what appeared to be a pile of clothes. Walking closer he realized it was Andy covered with the same old dusty blanket he'd covered Palmer with.

Dobbs nudged Andy, "Andy, wake up."

Skeeter rolled over on his bunk, "Wow. I must have gone out like a light. What's up?"

"You need to go to the mess hall and get something to eat."

"I don't feel much like eating."

"Come on, let's go, you gotta eat."

Skeeter got to his feet and he and Dobbs walked to the mess tent. Most of the workers were already eating their food. As Dobbs and Skeeter walked past, the workers would not look up or say anything. One person stood up and said, "Good going, Andy, you're an alright guy." He started to applaud Skeeter. All of a sudden all the workers stood up and clapped their hands and cheered for him. They realized if it were not for Skeeter, Palmer would be put in an unmarked grave and forgotten. They all hoped when they took the Westbound someone like Skeeter would be there for them.

Skeeter nodded his head, smiled, and sat down to eat his meal.

Dobbs, standing next to Skeeter, hit the table with a spoon and in a loud voice said, "Anyone that would like to attend Palmer's funeral tomorrow can. We will be leaving from the mess hall at eleven-fifteen. You should stop work at ten, clean up the best you can. We will give Palmer a good send-off." All the workers stood and again applauded.

The next day, Skeeter, Dobbs, Sam, and Charlie met at the mess hall at eleven o'clock. Charlie had already gotten the van to transport the workers to the funeral home.

One by one every worker showed up at the mess hall, all twenty-six of them. All the workers looked their best. The men were shaved, some for the first time in weeks, and dressed in the best clothes they had. They buttoned the top button of their

frayed collared shirts. The women had makeup on, some even wore a dress.

Dobbs was like an orchestra conductor waving and pointing, giving instructions, "Sam, you and Charlie go get the other van and pickup." Dobbs did not expect such a large crowd. They would need another vehicle.

When Sam and Charlie returned he said, "OK, folks, let's get started. The ladies will ride in the vans. The men will fill any empty seats in the van and the overflow will ride in the pickups."

Upon arriving at the Leonard Smalley Funeral Home the entourage of carny workers led by Dobbs and Skeeter were welcomed at the door by Roy. With a surprised look, he said, "Come in, come in." Roy immediately sought out Leonard Smalley who was in the viewing room along with Martha. "You gotta come quick! Andy and all the people from the carnival are here. What will we do with all of them?"

Martha, with great enthusiasm, told him, "Invite them in! You and Leonard get enough chairs to seat them. I will attend to the guests." Leonard and Roy left to get the chairs. Martha left for the lobby of the funeral home.

When entering the lobby, Martha smiled and in a cheerful voice exclaimed, "My, what a nice group of ladies and gentlemen to visit Mr. Palmer. Come this way," and she led the way to the viewing room where Palmer laid in repose.

Leonard and Roy were still setting up the chairs.

"Andy, you sit right here," Martha pointed to a chair in the middle of the first row. Skeeter sat down and motioned

Dobbs, Sam, and Charlie to chairs next to him, "You guys sit here." Before long everyone was seated.

Palmer never looked better. Shaved, wearing a new white shirt and tie, and a nice black sport coat. The twenty-dollar flowers rested at the foot of Palmer's casket. By the size of the flowers, Martha must have gotten a real buy.

All the carny workers looked around thinking *Not bad for a pauper's funeral.*

The preacher came in and gave a respectful but brief eulogy based on the lies Skeeter told on the forms. At the end of the eulogy, Mr. Smalley walked to the front of the viewing room and announced, "We will exit to the left. Proceed outside and drive to the cemetery."

Andy rode to the cemetery in a shiny white Cadillac that the Smalley Funeral Home used to drive family members of the deceased to and from the cemetery.

The drive took only fifteen minutes. Once there, the procession drove back to what appeared to be a small overgrown field. The procession stopped. Mr. Smalley got out of the lead car and motioned for everyone to follow him to Palmer's gravesite.

The preacher took his place at the head of the grave. Skeeter stood to his left, and everyone else not knowing exactly what to do, eventually found a place around the grave keeping their eyes on the ground. The hobos shifted anxiously considering the death of Palmer. They didn't talk about death, they simply referred to it as Taking the Westbound. When the preacher gave his final words the carny workers went back to their cars, vans, and trucks for their ride back to the carny.

Skeeter looked up after the preacher's prayer and saw a single set of railroad tracks less than fifty yards from Palmer's grave. Skeeter thought *How great is that, Palmer will be able to hear the trains go by.* He smiled and walked back to the limousine. On his way to the Cadillac, Leonard turned to Skeeter and said, “Andy, I will drive you back to the funeral home. Martha would like to say goodbye to you and afterward, I will drive you to the carnival.”

After arriving at the funeral home, Leonard and Skeeter were greeted by Martha. She walked over to Skeeter and hugged him. “Here, Andy, take this.” She handed him an envelope. Leonard and I would like you to have this. Don’t open it until you're back at the carnival and have a little time to rest. Good luck to you in whatever you pursue. You are a fine young man.”

With tears in her eyes, Martha turned and walked away. Leonard motioned toward the door, “OK. Let’s go.” They left the funeral home, got into the white Cadillac, and drove to the carnival.

Arriving at the carnival, Leonard asked “Where do you want me to let you off, Andy?”

“At the bunkhouse, “he said, pointing at a red semi-trailer, “over there.”

Pulling up to the bunkhouse Leonard stopped the car and said, “Martha will miss you. She sort of took a liking to you. I will miss you too. Here is my business card. If you have a chance, drop us a note. We would like to know what happens to Andy Miller, best friend of Dr. C. William Palmer.”

Skeeter got out of the white Cadillac limousine, looked back at Leonard, stuck out his hand, and said, “Thanks for

everything you and Mrs. Smalley did for Palmer. I will never forget it." The two shook hands. Skeeter turned and walked toward the bunkhouse. He never looked back as Leonard drove off.

Skeeter decided not to go directly to the bunkhouse. Instead, he sat at a picnic table. The day was cool but the sun was shining and there was a slight breeze. He just sat there for a moment trying not to think of anything. After a few minutes, he reached into his pocket and retrieved the envelope Martha had given him. He opened it and inside was a handwritten note along with one hundred fifty dollars.

The note read:

Andy,
It was so nice to meet you and help with the funeral of your friend, Dr. C. William Palmer. Please keep the money enclosed and use it to help you on your life's journey.

Sincerely,
Leonard and Martha Smalley

Skeeter broke down in tears and wept like a baby. All his emotions that had built up over the past months since the murders came pouring out in his tears. He put the note back in his pocket. Just then Dobbs showed up.

Dobbs said, taking his hat off, "You sure gave a good send-off to Palmer. He would be proud." He paused to put his hat back on. Becoming business-like again, he went on, "We will

be finishing the teardown tomorrow. Should be at the winter storage area about noon. It's only thirty or forty miles from here." Then turning to go he said, "See you in the morning, Andy."

Skeeter spent a restless night sleeping only to be awakened at seven a.m. by a banging on the bunkhouse door. "Come and get it while it's hot! Come on, you're burning daylight!" It was Sam starting the day as usual.

Everyone including Skeeter was up and out of the bunkhouse and over to the mess hall where the same food was on the menu. Oatmeal, bread, no butter, coffee black, no sugar.

No one said much to Skeeter, they just smiled, nodded their heads when he walked by. After breakfast, everyone went to work finishing the teardown, and then they were off.

Skeeter took his seat in the van with Dobbs, Sam, and Charlie. As they traveled on, his thoughts of Palmer came to him once again. Palmer's grave was marked with a bright shiny bronze marker for anyone to see. His grave was facing a railroad track. Who knows, maybe A-Number-One - the Muhammad Ali, the Babe Ruth of hobos - will pass by.

In forty-five minutes they arrived at the winter headquarters of the Dobbs' Carnival Show. It was nothing more than a big open field enclosed by a six-foot-high chain link fence. There were already a few carnival and circus companies stored up for the winter.

Dobbs pulled into the storage area first. He drove to a section that he used in the past. Getting out of his truck, Dobbs began directing where he wanted the other drivers to park, waving his hands this way and that, pointing here and there,

shaking his head, yes or no, until each semi-truck and van was in its proper place.

Dobbs motioned for everyone to gather around him. He then said, "It has been a long season. Not the most profitable but not bad. I would like to give each of you a bonus." The bonus was not very much. Dobbs said it depended on how long each person worked for him and on what kind of job they performed. Like their paychecks, it had nothing to do with how long or which job but was what Dobbs wanted to pay them.

Dobbs handed Sam and Charlie the envelopes with each worker's name on them to pass out. Dobbs went over to Andy and handed him two envelopes. One had "Andy" written on it the other had "Palmer". He said, "I think Palmer would want you to have his bonus." There was a quick look of surprise on Skeeter's face. He didn't expect that Dobbs would be this generous. He certainly didn't have to give Palmer's share to anyone. Dobbs continued, "Where are you going from here, Andy? You know you will always have a job with me. We will be hitting the road next April first, seven a.m. sharp."

"I don't know," Skeeter looked off to the south and sighed heavily, having no idea what lay ahead. "Maybe ride the rails in Florida until next spring. Right now I think I'll just walk into town and see what's going on. How far do you think it is?"

"Go through the entrance gate and hang a left at the next road. It leads right to town. About a mile or so."

"How big a town would you say it is?"

"Oh, about fifteen thousand."

"Bigger than the town I'm from," forgetting that he lied about being from South Bend. Dobbs did not pick up on the slip by Skeeter. It wouldn't have mattered anyway.

Skeeter flung his duffel bag over his shoulder, smiled, tipped his hat, and said, "Thanks for everything, Dobbs. I'll be seeing you around."

"See you around, Andy. Don't do anything I wouldn't do," Dobbs said, then to himself added, "I'm gonna miss that guy."

Skeeter, clean shaved, clothes washed and ironed turned and with a smile on his face said to himself, "Where are we going now, Palmer, where are we going? Go south and ride the rails or eat snowballs in the north?"

Skeeter was alone for the first time since he killed Anderson, Hicks, and Barns.

Chapter 18

It was just about noon as Skeeter walked through the entrance gate down to the next road and hung a left just as Dobbs said.

Not far into his walk Skeeter came upon a road to his right. It was not like the two-lane blacktop road leading to town. It was a one-lane dirt road. At the entrance was a weather-beaten wood sign that read ***Gibsonton's Poultry Farm ¼ mile***. The sign had an arrow at the bottom pointing south.

Looking down the road over an open field Skeeter could see three long buildings.

Skeeter thought to himself *A chicken farm just like the one I worked at back in Michigan.* Skeeter kept walking until he came to another big sign this one read, ***Gibsonton, Florida, population 15,526***. Skeeter wondered if every time someone was born or died they changed the number.

Walking farther Skeeter started to see the layout of this section of Gibsonton known as Gibtown which was a town within a town and was located on the west side of Gibsonton. Five thousand or so live there. Gibtown was considered the other side of the tracks. The people were less prosperous, less educated than main street Gibsonton.

Gibtown was once the home of a thriving ball-bearing manufacturing company that employed one hundred fifty people. It moved out twenty years ago and devastated the economy. The employees, for the most part, remained in Gibtown.

Skeeter noticed a restaurant here, a hardware there, a small supermarket over there. Just like back home. Not many buildings over two stories high. Another thing he noticed was the condition of the buildings. They all could use a coat of paint and some fixing up. Not much high scale anything.

Farther up the street he came to a bar with a help wanted sign. Faded red and white checkered curtains covered the store's big front window. On the window the name "Docs" with the O missing but you could still see the outline of the letter. The rest of the letters were cracking but clearly visible.

Skeeter opened the door and a little bell rang. He stepped inside, looked around, and saw two men sitting at a bar talking and sipping beer. Skeeter walked over to them. Not seeing anyone else he asked, "Do you know where the owner is?"

One of the men nodded and shouted out, "Doc, someone wants ya up here." The men continued talking and sipping their beer as if Skeeter wasn't there.

A moment later from the back of the bar came a short stout man, quite bald with just a little white hair around the sides

of his head. He was wearing a less than clean white apron covering just the lower half of his body. In his mouth was an unlit cigar. As he got close to Skeeter he smiled and said, "What can I do ya for?"

"Your sign out front. You need help, I need a job."

Doc replied, "You ever cooked in a bar before?"

"No, but I've eaten a lot of food in a bar."

Doc chuckled and asked, "Have you ever tended bar before?"

"No, but I drank a lot of beer in a bar before."

Doc laughed a little. Then with a serious look on his face, he said, "I don't know. The last couple guys stole money from the till and skipped out on me."

"Tell you what I'll do since I don't have any experience, let me work for a day, if it doesn't work out you don't need to pay me anything and I'm outta here."

Doc smiled and nodded with approval, then said, "You know, you just might work out." Then he went on, "The work is hard, you're on your feet a lot. The pay isn't very good. I can only pay a little over minimum."

Skeeter smiled back and said, "When do I start?"

"You started five minutes ago. I'll show you a few things before the rush."

Skeeter looked around the room. There were just the two men sitting at the bar, the same two that were there when he came in. He thought *What rush*?

Doc put out his hand and said, "I'm Doc Harris. My friends call me Doc. What's yours?"

Skeeter remembered what Palmer said: lie, lie, lie. He thought *I'm starting over, nothing from the past, no Skeeter, no Andy, nothing.* Skeeter said, "My name is C. William Palmer, my friends call me Palmer. The two men shook hands and laughed.

Doc motioned with his hand and said, "'C. William Palmer, my friends call me Palmer', follow me to the kitchen." As they started to walk, one of the men at the bar shouted out, "Hey, Doc, bring us another beer!"

"Come on, Palmer, you might just as well see where the keg is behind the bar." Doc pointed to a keg of beer that was already tapped for use. "Almost all the boys that come in here drink Coors, some will drink Millers," he nodded toward the other keg. "Do you know how to tap a keg?"

"Now that's something that I do know how to do!" They both laughed.

"The glasses are on this overhead rack." He took down two beer mugs and handed them to Skeeter. "Go ahead, pour the two beers and take them down to Paul and Tim. Paul is the one on the right."

"Do they pay each time or do they run a tab?"

"So you have been to a bar once or twice. They both run a tab. They settle up every Friday. When they have the money," he said with a shrug of the shoulders. "Come on, let's get back to the kitchen. It's a small area at the back of the bar."

There was a grill and a small work area on either side of the grill. In front of the grill, there was a board with holes in it where containers of mustard, ketchup, relish, and onions were located for easy access.

"This is it. Easy peasy nice and easy. Everything you need. You hardly have to move, and that's good because you can't." He opened the refrigerator door and pointed to several stacks of hamburger patties and said, "I prepare about three dozen patties every morning and put them in the fridge for later. There are also eggs, bacon, ham, and sausage. That'll be about ninety percent of what we sell here. There are a few other items you might use. I'll show you how to make my famous chili too. Most of the guys drink beer or wine. Once in a while whiskey straight up on the rocks or with soda. You'll catch on quick. Come in tomorrow around eleven A.M. and I will show you the ropes. Are you hungry?" Here Doc took two of the hamburger patties out of the refrigerator and threw them on the grill. "Might as well make your first order yours."

Skeeter was very hungry. It was mid-afternoon and he hadn't had a bite since breakfast. He thanked Doc and went to the grill, picked up a spatula, and started cooking. Skeeter got the hamburger buns out and laid them on the work area next to the grill.

Doc said, "Put the buns on the burgers and it'll warm them up. Makes them taste better. You'll learn, you'll learn," he laughed a little.

Skeeter finished cooking the burgers. Doc gestured to Skeeter to go to the bar so they could talk for a while. They walked a few steps and both sat down at one end of the long bar. Skeeter pushed one of the burgers to Doc.

Shaking his head, Doc said, "No, no. You eat both of them. I'm not hungry."

The front door opened and two more of the good ole boys came in and walked over to the bar. They said hello to Paul and Tim, still sipping their beers.

Doc stood up and said, “Let’s go, we got customers,” and he started walking to the front of the bar. Skeeter took one last big bite of his burger, wiped his mouth on his shirt sleeve, and trailed close behind Doc. As they got closer to the men, one of them held up two fingers.

“Got to learn sign language to work here. Get two Coors out of the cooler, these two aren’t weaned yet. They drink straight from the bottle.”

Skeeter got the two Coors and placed them in front of the new arrivals.

“This here is Palmer. He’s going to be helping with the bar. Palmer, this is Mike and Sid.”

They nodded and said hello. You had to look twice to tell the difference between Paul and Tim, and Sid and Mike. They all appeared to need a shave, were about the same age, and dressed about the same. On a social ladder, you would put the four of them one step above carny workers.

“If you guys want anything just give a holler. Palmer and I have some business to discuss.” Then tugging Skeeter’s sleeve Doc said, “Come on, Palmer, your other burger is getting cold.”

Doc and Palmer went back to the other end of the bar and Skeeter began eating his burger. In between bites, Skeeter asked, “So is there a Mrs. Doc?”

Doc, with a sigh, said, “Yeah. But not here anymore. We were married for about ten years. Had a little girl. I bought the

bar. Worked all the time, sixty hours a week, sometimes more. Nights, weekends." With a forlorn look, he said, "They left and moved to Georgia. I guess it just got to be too much for her. Brenda, that was my wife's name, died a few years ago. June, that's my daughter's name, she's all grown up now. Don't hear much from her anymore. Christmas card, birthday card once in a while, that's about it." Shifting direction, he asked, "What about you, Palmer? You must have had some kind of life before today." Doc had a good idea where Skeeter came from. For years circuses and carnivals wintered just outside of town, and it was that time of year. He also knew he'd never seen Skeeter before. Two and two came up Skeeter was a carny worker. The question might be too personal. "Would you rather not talk about it?"

"I didn't have much of a life." *Remember, Skeeter: lie, lie, lie.* "I was born and raised in a small town just outside of Philadelphia, Pennsylvania, about the same size as Gibsonton actually. I spent a three-year hitch in the Army, returned home, got married, had three kids, and got a divorce. Left a while back and I wound up here." Skeeter has learned to live with a lie. You have to have a certain amount of truth in a lie or it just won't work. Skeeter remembered what the real Palmer had told him about his hometown. He would have to use the information left in Palmer's billfold - driver's license, birth certificate, and social security card - if he is to continue to be Palmer. He would need this information to fill out an employment application that Doc would ask him to complete, as well as apply for a new driver's license if needed or for whatever documents he would have to fill out in the future. Yes, Skeeter was becoming good at this lying thing.

A moment later the bell over the front door rang. This time it wasn't one of the good ole boys, it was a woman. She immediately took off her coat, flung it over her shoulder with a bounce to her step, and started walking toward Doc and Skeeter. On her way by she looked toward the men at the bar, smiled, waved, and said, "How you all doin?" The men at the bar nodded, grunted hello, and continued sipping their beer.

When she arrived where Doc and Skeeter were sitting she walked past them to the kitchen area where she took a red and white checkered apron off a hook beside the refrigerator. She turned around and looked at Doc and said, "Who do we have here?"

"Beverly, I would like you to meet C. William Palmer, his friends call him Palmer. Palmer, this is Beverly. Her friends call her Beverly."

Beverly was a good-looking redhead with blue eyes and was very well built. I mean, very well built. She wore her clothes a little too tight. She might be a size twelve but she wore a size ten. And she looked nice doing it.

"Palmer is going to be helping us around the bar. Cook a little, tend the bar a little."

"It's about time you got someone to help out around here." Beverly asked skeptically, "Where are you from? Ever tend bar before, ever cook before?"

Laughing, Doc said, "No, but he's eaten and drank in a bar before. There will be plenty of time to get to know each other."

The bell over the front door of the bar rang several times in the last few minutes.

"Beverly, we better get going. Palmer, stick with me, it's going to get busy." The little bell over the door was just about to ring off the hook. All three started walking to the front. Skeeter couldn't believe his eyes. It was as if someone unloaded a bus full of people in front of the bar. "Where did all these people come from?"

Beverly removed her pencil and order pad from her apron and started moving toward the tables in the front of the bar. The crowd was getting loud. From over her shoulder, she answered Skeeter, "From the bowling alley across the street. Be happy it's Sunday. Friday and Saturday we get two leagues of bowlers and the crowds are bigger. Most of them are already half pie-eyed when they get here and the other half wants to be."

The little bar was soon overflowing with people. All the seats around the bar were taken and the tables were full. Everyone called out their orders at the same time. "Burger with everything!", "Burger no onions!", "Bowl of chili!". Beverly wrote the food orders as fast as she could.

Doc was frantic. "Palmer, go back to the kitchen and start cooking. Throw on a dozen patties; make sure you put the buns on top."

"How do I know what to put on 'em?"

"Make them with everything, and then put the finished burgers on the paper plates like I showed you. While you're cooking, serve up a dozen or so bowls of chili. When you get that done, do it all over again. That will take care of most of the orders, after that you can start the special orders Beverly gives you."

Beverly took the burgers and bowls of chili that Skeeter prepared, placed them on a large tray, and danced through the bar like a ballerina calling out "Who has a burger with everything?" and "Who has a chili?" At the same time, customers yelled back, "I have two burgers!", "I have a burger and a chili!", "I need a beer!"

Fifteen minutes later the bar seemed to calm down. Most were eating something they may or may not have ordered. It didn't matter. Most of them were too hungry or too drunk to care. Beverly started taking special orders back to Skeeter.

During the mayhem Doc was drawing beer from a keg, all of the beer was Coors. He would put beer on the bar where Beverly would pick them up. Randomly he would make up whiskey drinks knowing someone would drink them. Whiskey straight up, on the rocks, with soda, all cheap house whiskey.

After thirty minutes the rush was over. The men were talking, laughing, shooting pool, and playing cards. Every now and then someone would shout out "in need of another beer" or "I need a burger with…"

Around midnight the men started filing out of the bar. The night's work was done. When the last of the bowlers left, Doc and Beverly, exhausted, dragged themselves back to the kitchen.

There he stood. Sleeves rolled partway up. Hair messed up, sweat dripping off the end of his nose. Mustard, ketchup, and relish were all over the front of him, on his face, arms, and the half apron he was wearing was covered.

Doc and Beverly had to laugh. Doc pointing at Skeeter said, "You should have worn a full apron!"

Beverly chimed in, "Looks like you've been rode hard and put away wet."

With a sheepish grin, Skeeter replied, "When I walked into this nice quiet bar I had no idea what I was getting myself into."

"Like I said before, Fridays and Saturdays are worse. They bowl two leagues, an early one that starts about six, and the late one starts about nine. Some of the six o'clock guys stay around and drink with the nine o'clock guys. It's a long hard night," Beverly said. Then she turned to leave, "Well, boys, I'm going to put this body to bed. I have been pinched, poked, and slapped enough for one night. See you guys tomorrow." She picked her coat from a hanger in the kitchen and started for the front door. She didn't leave but stayed back and sat at the end of the bar.

Doc said to Skeeter in a low voice, "She's a very nice person. I couldn't run the place without her."

Skeeter removed his ketchup and mustard-stained apron using it to wipe off his face, "She seems to know what she's doing alright."

"You're going to be alright. Got a place to stay?

"Yeah, I'm good. Did I pass the test? Do you want me to come back tomorrow?"

Doc's unlit cigar all but chewed to pieces, his belly bouncing with laughter, said, "You sure did. Be here tomorrow and make it about noon. You already have a good jump on things. I just need to show you how to prepare for the day."

The two men shook hands. Skeeter got his coat and left out the back door.

Beverly was quite a savvy woman. She lived in Gibsonton all of her life. She's worked for Doc for the past five years. She knows who is and who isn't, she knows Skeeter isn't. She knows every year about this time the carnivals and circuses park their equipment just outside of town. From time to time the carny workers come into town. One day out of the blue Palmer shows up at Doc's Bar and wants a job as a cook in a run-down bar. Beverly had Skeeter pegged perfectly. From her seat at the end of the bar, while lighting up a cigarette, Beverly said to Doc, "You know he's a bum, don't you? He's probably living out there where the carnivals and circuses park their junk for the winter."

"He seems like a nice guy. All he needs is a chance."

On her way out of the bar, she said, "Don't say I didn't tell you."

On his way back to the bunkhouse with a smile on his face and a twinkle in his eye, Skeeter started to reflect on the day. *I think I might have found a home at last. Doc doesn't ask too many questions and Beverly seems to be alright. What a day.*

As he came to the place he had stashed his duffel bag for safekeeping, he looked around cautiously, and seeing no one, he picked up his belongings and continued on to the bunkhouse.

Once there he opened the door and looked around suspiciously, wondering *Anyone here? Who are they?* He entered the bunkhouse, his duffel bag hanging at his side. There was no light. Waiting a moment for his eyes to adjust to the darkness, he noticed five or six men sleeping but he did not recognize any of them because it was so dark. Skeeter thought *I better sleep with both eyes open tonight*. He picked out a bunk at

the front left corner of the trailer. There he chose the bottom bunk giving him more concealment from a predator approaching. He would have the wall of the trailer at his back and a clear view of the rest of it. A perfect location. A bunk in the back in the corner in the dark. Remember what Palmer said, "You can trust no one ever".

Very quietly Skeeter put his duffel bag on the floor, rolled out his bedding, and put it on the bunk. He lay down, pulled up his worn-out blanket, remembering his first night with the carnival, and placed his pistol under the blanket. He was so tired from the busy night at the bar he fell asleep almost instantly.

The next morning Skeeter was awakened with a start. Some of the men were getting ready for the day.

Now with the light of the open door, he recognized a couple of the men from Dobbs' Carnival. One was called Smithy the other Handsome, as you might imagine Handsome wasn't so handsome. He was described by many of his fellow hobo friends as "having a face like a pan full of worms". Apparently Handsome had been in a fire sometime in his life.

Smithy and Handsome walked over and greeted Skeeter. They were all smiles patting Skeeter on the back and shaking his hand as if they had just met a long-lost friend. One of them said, "Andy, we thought you would be gone by now riding the rails in Florida."

Skeeter, not all that enthused about seeing them, reluctantly pulled out his right hand from under the cover. He forgot he still held the pistol from last night. The two men

jumped back when they saw it. Skeeter said, "Oh, I'm sorry about that, can't be too careful, you know."

The two men smiled as if to say everything is OK. Smithy did most of the talking. He was the smarter of the two. He had an I.Q. of maybe seventy-five. He asked, "Where've you been? What's your plans?"

Skeeter definitely did not want to reveal what he was doing or where he was going and said, "Don't have any plans right now. I think I'll stick around another day or so."

With the tip of his hat Smithy said, "Come on, Handsome, we better hit the rails south." Then to Skeeter, he said, "We'll see you around, Andy. Maybe next spring."

Handsome chimed in, "Yeah, maybe spring." Smithy and Handsome left the trailer leaving Skeeter alone.

Chapter 19

It was about ten-thirty A.M. when Skeeter looked at his railroad pocket watch Mary Lou gave him. Skeeter, with a longing feeling and a lump in his throat, said aloud, "How long has it been? A million years or more?" He put the watch back in his pocket, picked up his bedroll, and put it in the duffel bag. He threw it over his shoulder and headed out for Doc's Bar.

Just on the outskirts of Gibsonton, Skeeter came to the place where he hid his duffel bag the day before. Looking around and not seeing anyone, he hid it again. He got back on the road and in no time was walking through the door of Doc's Bar.

Once inside he started for the back of the bar where the kitchen was. He looked over toward the bar and there sat Paul and Tim talking and sipping beer as if they never left. As Skeeter passed by the two of them, he said, "Good morning, boys."

Without looking up or missing a sip of their beer they both nodded and grunted, "Hi."

When Skeeter arrived at the kitchen, Doc was already there. "You're a little early."

While hanging up his coat Skeeter said, "Better early than late."

Doc clapped his hands together, "Let's get started." He opened the refrigerator door and pulled out a large package of ground beef and placed it on the work area next to the grill. "First, we'll make up the hamburger patties." He pulled a round contraption that was made up of two pieces of wood, each piece was about five inches in diameter and an inch thick; they were hinged together so they could be opened and closed without falling apart. Next, he got a spoon out from a shelf under the grill. It looked like a large ice cream scoop. He reached onto the top shelf again and brought down a box of wax paper pre-cut into five-inch squares. He opened the round contraption, placed a piece of wax paper on the bottom, picked up a scoopful of ground beef and placed it on the paper, closed the two pieces together, pushed down, and said, "Voila! And there you have it, a perfect hamburger patty every time. When you're done, put them in the fridge. Think you can handle it?"

"I think I got it."

"Do that about forty times."

Doc reached back into the refrigerator and pulled out another large package of ground beef. He put it on the grill and said, "This will make about forty bowls of chili." He added mustard, opened a can of mushrooms, cut them up, added chili powder, a tablespoon of Uncle Jack's Hot Pepper Sauce, two

large cans of hot chili beans, two large cans of diced chili tomatoes, and one medium-sized diced white onion. "Mix them all together." Then he put all the cooked ingredients into a crockpot. "We do this every day, but on Friday and Saturday we double the amount."

Doc, rubbing his rather large belly, said. "I'm getting hungry, how about you? Why don't you serve us up a couple bowls of chili and fry up a couple hamburger patties? We can have lunch."

"Sounds good to me." Doc sat on a stool close to the grill.

"After we eat you can fill out the employment application. Won't take long."

"Sure thing." Skeeter served up the chili and burger. *Remember, Skeeter, when you fill out the employment application, lie, lie, lie.*

After wolfing down the burger and chili, Doc asked, "How is your living arrangement going?"

"OK. I'm looking for something better."

The bell over the front door rang. It was Beverly ready for the day. She removed her coat, flung it over her shoulder, waved to Paul and Tim sitting at the bar, and said, "How are you doin', boys?" They grunted and nodded their heads and continued sipping beer. Beverly walked to the kitchen and put her coat on a hanger. She whipped on the not-so-clean red and white checkered apron. She turned to go to the head of the bar. On her way she called out, "Come on, guys, let's head 'em up, let's move 'em out." Skeeter with a spatula in one hand and a chili bowl in the other said, "Bring 'em on."

Doc shook his head and smiled as he followed Beverly saying to himself, "I have never had this much fun running the bar."

The little bell over the door rang continually. The evening started with the bowlers coming in hollering to the top of their voices, "A burger with everything!", "A bowl of chili!", and "I need a beer!" After an hour or so, things calmed down. Everyone was gone except Paul and Tim sitting at the same place sipping beer and grunting something when someone said hello or goodbye.

Each night was the same as the one before except Friday and Saturday, they were busier then. Each night Skeeter got a little better at his job. Part of his daily routine included walking Beverly to her apartment which was located above a hardware store on the corner of Main and Hickory. They both would say good night and Skeeter would continue to the bunkhouse.

Fridays were bad, but this one was worse. All hell broke loose. The first shift of bowlers came in then the second shift. It didn't look like the first shift ever left. All the prepped food was gone and now in a flurry, Palmer had to make more burgers from scratch.

Finally, the last of the bowlers left. Beverly and Skeeter took off their aprons, put on their coats, bid good night to Doc, and left the bar. When they arrived at the corner of Main and Hickory, Skeeter started to say good night but Beverly interrupted him and said, "Would you like to come up for a cup of coffee?"

"Sure, I could use a good hot cup of coffee."

That was probably the best cup of coffee Skeeter ever had. As a matter of fact, he had several cups of coffee that night.

After staying at Beverly's for two or three nights, Skeeter woke one morning to see Beverly cooking breakfast. Sitting on the side of the bed getting ready for the day, Skeeter asked, "Is there an apartment above the bar?"

"What's the matter, this place isn't good enough?" Beverly gave him a sideways look with a spatula in hand.

"I've been on the road a long time. I just need a place of my own for a while."

"Yeah, there's an apartment, but it hasn't been used in a long time."

"I think I'm going to ask Doc if I can rent it."

"He won't."

"You want to bet?"

"How much?"

Skeeter motioned for Beverly to sit on his lap. And she did. "I'll bet you five bucks."

"You're on."

And Skeeter had another cup of coffee.

After breakfast, Skeeter left for the bar. On his way to the kitchen, he waved and said hello to Paul and Tim sitting at their usual spot sipping beer. Doc was already in the kitchen. He looked up when he saw Skeeter and said, "You're early."

"Yeah." Then with a serious look said, "There's something I would like to talk over with you."

"Nothing wrong, is there?"

"No, no, nothing like that. I just wanted to ask you about the apartment above the bar. I would like to rent it."

"I don't know, Palmer. Brenda and I lived there the first seven or eight years we were married. Brought June home from the hospital there after she was born." When Doc said this he seemed reflective. But then with a bitter tone, he added, "I tried renting it a couple of times. Renters didn't pay the rent. Had to go to the courts. It was just a mess."

"You won't go through all that with me. You can take the rent out of my pay. If I don't take care of the apartment, you can fire me. I'll pay whatever you say. I just need a place to stay."

Doc knew where Skeeter had been spending the last few nights. Doc asked tongue in cheek, "What's the matter with the place you're staying now?"

Skeeter knew that Doc knew where he was staying at night. It was one of those I know - you know things. "The coffee is great but the place is too small."

"Alright, I'll give you a chance. I don't want to lose you as an employee and a friend over a rundown old apartment."

"You won't, I promise. It's about an hour or so before my start time. Can we go up and take a look?"

Doc looked down to the end of the bar where Paul and Tim were sitting sipping a beer. Knowing the bar wasn't going to get busy in the next ten minutes, Doc motioned for Skeeter to follow him to a narrow enclosed stairway behind the bar which led to the apartment. Pulling out a ring of keys he fumbled a moment. "Oh yeah, it's this one," he said as he put it in the keyhole. "Don't expect much, it's been a while since anyone has lived here."

Doc opened the door and flipped on a light that shone dimly over the stairway leading up. Once at the door of the apartment Doc reached inside the door and turned on a light which revealed the living room of the apartment. Doc and Skeeter entered the room and started looking around. The living room contained a sofa, easy chair, coffee table, two end tables, and an old TV in the corner. The floor was covered by a large, very dirty, very worn throw rug. Peeking out around the edges of the rug was the old unfinished wood floor.

Looking further into the apartment, Skeeter saw there was a half wall at one end of the living room which revealed a small dining area and kitchen on the other side of it. The dining area had a table and four chairs. In the kitchen was a stove, refrigerator, sink, cupboards, and all were a dirty faded white. The floor of the dining area and kitchen was a worn black and white checkered linoleum.

To the right of the living room were two bedrooms complete with beds and nightstands. Between the two bedrooms was a bathroom with stool, sink, and bathtub with a shower.

There were boxes everywhere, all over the floors, sofa, beds, tables, and chairs. Doc was using the apartment for a storage area for the bar.

After looking things over, Skeeter turned to Doc, smiled, and said, “It's beautiful. I love it. I’ll take it.”

Doc with a sober expression said, “You must have come from some mighty rough digs.”

“It's an hour or so before I clock in. Can I stay and start cleaning up?”

"Sure, just take the stuff for the bar and put it into the garage next to the bar. I'll sort it all out later. I'm going to go down and see if Paul or Tim need another beer."

Just before the evening rush, in popped Beverly. She removed her coat and flung it over her shoulder, walked past Paul and Tim, waved and said, "How ya doin', boys?" and continued to the kitchen where Doc was.

"Where's Palmer?" asked Beverly nonchalantly.

Doc pointed straight up. "Upstairs cleaning."

Beverly's eyes widened and she stopped everything, "You rented Palmer the apartment?!"

"Yep."

"Damn, you cost me five bucks. It's still a little while before start time. Do you care if I go up and see what's going on?"

"No, go ahead. Give him a hand."

Beverly turned to go up to the apartment. Doc, with a chuckle in his voice, said, "What do you think of that bum now?"

Beverly continued on her way and without looking at Doc, replied, "You're getting funnier every day, Doc."

At the top of the stairs, she stopped and knocked on the door. From inside Skeeter hollered, "Come in!"

Beverly opened the door and walked in a few feet then stopped and said, "This place is a mess."

Skeeter was in the dining area with a mop and a pail. He looked at Beverly and said, "You should have seen it an hour ago." He put his mop down, walked over to Beverly, kissed her,

and said, "Where's my five bucks?" He then added, "Are you here to clean or what?"

"Or what!"

"No time for or what. Can you take one of those boxes downstairs to the garage? I'll follow you with a couple more. It's just about time to start work." They picked up boxes and headed to the garage.

Upon returning to the bar, they put on their aprons and started working.

Doc came over to them and asked, "How's it going?"

Skeeter answered, "Great! I see you have an old Packard in the garage."

With a bit of regret, Doc said, "Yeah, I haven't driven it in years. You ought to take it for a drive sometime, Palmer."

Beverly could not believe her ears. First, Doc rented the apartment to Palmer, and now, he asks him if he wants to drive his prized possession. Doc let few people even see the Packard let alone drive it.

"No. I would be afraid I might scratch it up. Besides, my driver's license expired a long time ago."

Doc said, "You should get a new driver's license so you can drive if you need to or to use for an I.D."

"I wouldn't know where to go." Not wanting to start that process.

"Go down to the DMV and get one. It's located right here in town. Gibsonton is the county seat. All county offices and some state offices are located there. DMV, welfare office, county police, we even have a branch of the state police here."

Skeeter thought to himself *Great! Local police, county police, state police. Are you sure the F.B.I. isn't here too?*

Beverly joined in, "I'll go with you. We can catch the GIB."

"What's the GIB?"

"GIB. It's the local bus line. You can go anywhere in the county for a small fee. The buses aren't very big, they only hold twelve people or so, it's more like a van. I'll call for one tomorrow at ten o'clock."

Skeeter was getting a little nervous, "I don't know."

Doc noticed the change in Skeeter's demeanor, "Don't worry, Palmer. There are a lot of people that have expired driver's licenses and need them renewed."

"OK, that's settled. Tomorrow at ten. While we're out we might as well pick up some things for your apartment," Beverly said with enthusiasm.

"Like what?"

"Like sheets, blankets, pillowcases. You know, stuff."

"Sounds like you're getting a little domesticated, Palmer," Doc said teasingly.

Chapter 20

The next morning Skeeter was awakened by Beverly. "Rise and shine, big boy! It's off to the DMV then shop till you drop. Sounds great huh?"

Skeeter rolled out of bed sleepy-eyed. "It sounds like one miserable day."

After breakfast, they were down the stairs of Beverly's apartment and standing on the corner of Main and Hickory waiting for the GIB. Within a few minutes, the GIB bus arrived. The driver opened the door and Beverly and Skeeter climbed aboard. The bus driver asked, "Where to?"

Beverly answered, "The DMV."

The driver informed them, "I have a couple stops to make along the way. Be there in half an hour or so."

Beverly looked around the bus walking ahead of Skeeter and found two seats together. "Let's sit here." There were four

other people on the bus. A woman and what looked to be her four-year-old daughter, a woman by herself, and a man she recognized from the bar. Beverly said hello to him. He replied, "Hello, Bev."

The bus driver dropped off the two women and a couple more passengers got on. Finally, pulling up to the government complex, the driver announced, "DMV."

Beverly and Skeeter got off the bus and started for the DMV. Skeeter noticed across the street from the DMV was the county sheriff's department and jail. At the far end of the government complex was the state police post. Skeeter thought *Great! County police, county jail, state police. Now I have to lie to the Department of Motor Vehicles.* Beverly and Skeeter entered the DMV.

Beverly walked over to a machine and pulled out a piece of paper with a number on it. She walked back to Skeeter, handed the paper to him, and said, "This place is like a meat market. Take a number and have a seat. Here, you're number seventeen. Let's take a seat over there." Skeeter was very nervous. He started to sweat and was wiggling his feet."

A voice said, "Number twelve." Every time a number was called, Skeeter jumped. A while later he heard, "Number seventeen."

Beverly nudged him, "That's you, Palmer."

Skeeter got up from his chair and walked to the counter. A middle-aged lady with a pleasant smile said, "What can I help you with today?"

In a slow stammering voice Skeeter said, "I need to renew my driver's license. I'm long overdue. I…"

The lady interrupted, "That's OK. Let me have your old license. We will see what we can do."

Skeeter handed her Palmer's old, very worn driver's license, social security card, and birth certificate. There were no questions about the picture on the license matching Skeeter's face because it was so worn out and faded. She said, "I think all I need for right now is your old license." She handed Skeeter back his social security card and birth certificate. "Take this form, go over to one of the tables, fill it out, and bring it back when you're finished."

Skeeter took the form, found an empty place at a table, and started filling out the form. *Remember, Skeeter, lie, lie, lie.*

> Name: Clare W. Palmer. That was Palmer's name on the old driver's license.
> Address: 211½ South Main Street
> City and State: Gibsonton, Florida
> Zip code: 39278.
> Do you have any of the following: NO, NO, NO.
> Have you ever had your driver's license revoked for any reason: NO.

He signed at the bottom *Clare W. Palmer* and took it back to the lady at the counter. She said, "OK. Have a seat. I will be right back with you."

Skeeter returned to his seat next to Beverly. "Now that wasn't so bad, was it?"

Skeeter was uneasy. What was taking so long? He started shaking his foot and squirming around a little.

Beverly noticed Skeeter's strange behavior, "What's the matter with you? Got ants in your pants? You're worse than a kid getting his first haircut."

"Mr. Clare Palmer." It was the lady he had been working with.

Skeeter got up from his seat. His legs were shaking but somehow managed to walk to the counter. She said, "Step to your left and smile. We will take your picture and in a few minutes you will have your new driver's license."

Skeeter stepped to his left and gave his best Skeeter smile.

"Great. I will call you when your license is ready."

When Skeeter sat next to Beverly again, he still had a smile on his face. Feeling much calmer he said, "That wasn't so bad."

Beverly smiled back, "What did you expect?"

The lady called his name, "Mr. Palmer." Skeeter got up and went over to the counter. "Here is your new State of Florida driver's license. Drive safely, Mr. Palmer." Skeeter looked at his license, thanked her, and returned to Beverly.

Looking at her watch Beverly said, "We may be in luck. The bus comes by this plaza every half hour. It's eleven-twenty. Let's go."

They left the plaza and ten minutes later the bus arrived just like clockwork. As they entered the bus Beverly said to the driver, "Corner of Main and Hickory." The bus was nearly full so they stood at one of the handrails. As people got off they eventually got a seat. When the bus approached the corner of Main and Hickory, Beverly pulled the cord that alerted the driver

to stop. From the bus, they went to Doc's to show him Skeeter's new driver's license, which Skeeter never stopped looking at from the time he got it.

When they got to the bar Beverly opened the door and saw Paul and Tim sitting in their usual spots. She asked Paul, "Where's Doc?" Without looking up from his beer he said, "In the kitchen." Beverly and Skeeter proceeded to the kitchen where Doc was getting things around for the day.

In her best impersonation of Bugs Bunny, Beverly said, "What's up, Doc?" He didn't look up from his work or say a word. She went on, "Palmer wants to show you his new license. He's prouder of it than if you bought him a new bicycle."

Doc wiped his hands on his apron. "Let's see." Beaming with pride, Palmer handed his new license to Doc.

Skeeter said, "Great picture, huh?"

Doc looked at the picture then at Skeeter and back at the picture, then at Skeeter again, and said with a laugh, "Looks like a wanted poster! Now, you're legal!"

Doc's statement "Looks like a wanted poster" took the smile off Skeeter's face, but only for a moment.

Skeeter never stopped looking at his license. He seemed to be happier about getting this one than he did about his first driver's license back in Michigan. Doc's words rang in his ear. "Now you're legal". That meant a lot.

Beverly said, "Come on, Palmer, put that license away. You look more at it than you do me."

Chapter 21

In early February, Palmer had been with Doc and Beverly for a short time. He got a job at the bar, got his own apartment, got a new driver's license, and Beverly moved into his apartment. He had established himself quite well. He had made a lot of friends.

One day, Palmer showed up for work earlier than usual. While Doc was busy getting ready for the day, Palmer asked a question from out of the blue, "Say, Doc, that building next door, was it a restaurant at one time?"

Doc continued to work without looking up, "Yeah."

"What do you know about it? Who owns the building?"

Not missing a beat, "I do. I ran a restaurant there for a short time."

"So what happened?"

"It took up a lot of my time. Didn't turn much of a profit. That was about the time Brenda and I split."

"Looks like a nice location, right on the corner of Main and Hickory. I think we should open a nice family-style restaurant. You know, meatloaf, scalloped potatoes, and ham, pork chops, chicken, that sort of thing."

Doc looked up at Skeeter. "You got a mouse in your pocket? Who is this 'we' you always talk about? Every time you say 'we' it means me."

"Hiring me, renting me the apartment. That worked out, didn't it?"

"I don't know. I paid for the paint, new flooring, new curtains, light fixtures. I gave you the apartment rent-free."

"The place needed a facelift and you gave me the apartment instead of a raise."

Doc chuckled a little, "Well, I'll have to think it over."

The bell at the door rang and Beverly came bouncing in. Off with her coat. She flung it over her shoulder and headed for the kitchen. On her way, she waved to Paul and Tim at the bar and said, "How are you doin', boys?" They nodded their heads and grunted. It's just deja vu all over again.

When Beverly arrived at the kitchen, Palmer asked, "What do you think about starting up a restaurant in the building next door on the corner of Main and Hickory?

Beverly stopped in her tracks and threw her hands in the air, "Are you kidding? Too much work!"

To this, Doc laughed some more and said, "That's what I said."

"Thanks for your support," Skeeter said unenthusiastically.

Beverly asked Skeeter, "Are you really thinking about opening a restaurant there?"

Doc chimed in, "No, he is thinking of 'we' opening a restaurant there. Him and the mouse he's got in his pocket. He wants me and probably you to open it with him."

"You think we could make a go of it?" Beverly asked Skeeter.

Doc rolled his eyes," There you go again with that 'we'."

"I'll tell you what. I don't have much money laid away. My employer doesn't pay me much," Skeeter humorously aimed at Doc, "but I will put it all up, all of it."

"Me too," Beverly offered.

Putting his hands on the bar, looking at the two of them, Doc said, "You haven't got a dollar thirty-five between the two of you. Let me think about it for a couple days. Now, let's go to work so we might be able to afford a restaurant next door."

A week went by. Doc, Palmer, and Beverly were working in the kitchen. "Palmer, how much thought have you put into this restaurant thing?" Doc asked.

"A lot," he answered. His eyes lit up when he thought about his plan, "I have gone through the place. It's not in bad shape at all. It needs a little paint, a good cleaning, and it's ready to go. It looks like the stove, refrigerator, and dishwasher are all in good shape. Everything else seems to be in place. Dishes, forks, knives, spoons, tables, chairs, booths are all in good condition. Clean it up and you would think it never closed." Pointing at a common wall between the bar and the proposed restaurant, "We could knock a hole between the bar and

restaurant. The customers could go back and forth. I don't think it would take much to get a beer, wine, and liquor license for the place. You already have one for the bar."

"I guess you really have given it some thought. What about the help? You need to get a good cook. Someone to manage the place. Hire wait staff. It's a pretty big project. I won't have much time for it," Doc informed Skeeter.

Skeeter started to believe his vision of a restaurant just might come true. "Beverly and I can clean the place up. We can hire a good cook. I will manage the place and Beverly can take care of training and managing the wait staff. You can take care of the money.

"What about the bar? You're taking my cook and waitress away!"

"Beverly and I will run the restaurant. She will run the day-to-day operation of the wait and cooking staff. I will take care of the business part and help out anywhere I can. I will see to it that you get a good person to replace both of us," Skeeter assured Doc.

"Look. You and Beverly get here an hour or so early tomorrow. We'll go over to the restaurant together. If the equipment is in as good a shape as you say, we may have a deal. I can't afford to replace anything. This is business, Palmer, it all has to be put down in writing."

"I wouldn't have it any other way."

The next morning, even before Paul and Tim got there, Skeeter and Beverly were at the bar ready to go inspect the restaurant with Doc.

Doc said apprehensively, "OK, let's go inspect the place." When they arrived, he opened the door. Inside Doc stopped, turned to Palmer, and said, "How did you get in here to check the place out? You didn't have a key."

"Where there is a will, there's a way," he responded.

Doc not knowing what to say to that comment said, "Let's check out the kitchen first. If the big stuff like the stove, fridge, and dishwasher check out we might be in business." After looking the kitchen area over, Doc said, "Everything looks good on the surface. Let me call the gas and electric company. We will come back and turn everything on. If that works, Palmer, I would say we have a deal."

Two days later the gas and electric company showed up at the restaurant and turned on the power.

Doc, Palmer, and Beverly went to the restaurant. Inside Doc flipped a switch for the lights. Light flooded the room. "Lights work." All three walked straight for the kitchen. Without saying a word Doc turned on the gas to the stove. Poof! He turned toward the other two and said, "Stove works." He opened the door to the refrigerator, the little light inside was on and you could hear the refrigerator motor running. "Refrigerator works." Doc looked at Skeeter and said, "Just a moment." He pushed the button on the dishwasher. They could hear the sound of water entering the machine. "Looks like we're in business! Let's go back to the bar. Palmer, you and I have business to discuss. Beverly, you take care of things at the bar."

When they got to the front entrance of the bar, guess who was waiting for them. Paul and Tim were anxiously waiting to enter the bar to start talking and sipping beer. "Give me room

to unlock the door, boys," Doc said as he stepped inside the bar. Paul and Tim made their way to the barstools they normally sat at. Beverly put on her apron, drew two mugs of Coors from the keg, and delivered them to Paul and Tim. They drank them straight down without coming up for air. They were minutes behind their schedule of talking and sipping beer. Wiping their lips on their shirt sleeves they nodded at Beverly for another. Doc and Skeeter walked back to the kitchen. Doc went to the work area next to the grill and picked up a large envelope then came back to Skeeter. He opened the envelope and took out a bunch of legal-looking documents. He gave one of them to Palmer.

"Here you go, Palmer, this one's for you."

Palmer looked at the papers and asked, "What's this?"

"Contracts between you and me. I told you this is business. Everything in writing so there will be no misunderstandings in the future. I may not be too bright, but I don't do anything without talking to my lawyer and accountant. Let's take a moment and read through these papers. You have any questions, ask. Take the papers home with you, read them over again. Come tomorrow and ask more questions. I want you to be sure you understand what you are getting into before you sign them."

"I will sign them now. You're not going to cheat me, are you?"

"I was told by someone, I can't remember who, don't make any big decisions until you've thought it over for twenty-four hours. Get reading, Palmer."

Palmer started reading the contract to himself. Party of the first part. Party of the second part on this day, and so forth. He stopped reading and said, "Does this mean that both you and I will share equally in the profits of said business?"

"Do you want more?"

"I don't want any. I just want to manage the restaurant and get a good pay."

"I keep telling you, Palmer, this is a business arrangement. You do all the work, I put up the money. You manage the restaurant and I will take care of the business end. Every week we will go over what happened during the week. You show me the sales receipts and expenses. I will write checks for everything. Bills, payroll, everything."

"It says that if anything happens to you, I get the restaurant and the bar. That's not right. Why would you give me the bar? What about your daughter?"

"Look, Palmer, I don't have anyone. My wife, Brenda, passed away. My daughter, June, never sees me or writes. I haven't known you very long but I do feel close to you. I believe you're a good man. I don't know much about your past, and I don't want to. Don't worry about my daughter. I talked things over with my lawyer and accountant. In order to protect your portion of the business, I bought business life insurance that will buy out her interest in the bar and restaurant in the event I die. The restaurant will pay for the insurance premium. I don't know what you want to do with Beverly, but the restaurant and bar are just between you and me. I know you will treat her fairly." Doc paused a moment then went on, "The restaurant will be a small corporation known as Palmer's Place. Above the entrance to the

restaurant will be a neon sign in green and red spelling out Palmer's Place. The bar is already incorporated, it's named Doc's Bar & Grill.

Skeeter was amazed at the business knowledge that Doc had. He just thought that Doc was a good ole hard-working guy who just happened to own a bar. "You may not be well educated, Doc, but you sure are business savvy. Why do you want to call the restaurant Palmer's Place?"

"You're getting to be pretty well known around town, people like ya. That will help with the business. Besides, I want to keep the bar and restaurant separate."

Over the next several days, Skeeter and Beverly worked all their awake hours either cleaning and fixing up the restaurant or working in the bar. They put down new tile flooring and hung new curtains. One major renovation was knocking a hole in the wall between the bar and the restaurant to allow customers to go back and forth.

Skeeter ran ads in the *Gibtown Independent,* a paper with a circulation of five thousand or so, asking for experienced wait staff and a cook. The owner of the paper was a woman by the name of Sherri Peterson. She received a degree in journalism from Florida State University. Her ambition was to work at a large newspaper in Little Rock, but one summer break she went back to Gibsonton and fell in love with Tom. They bought the hardware and later Sherri started the paper. They both became business leaders in the Gibtown section of Gibsonton.

Beverly interviewed the wait staff applicants, and Skeeter and Beverly both interviewed the cooks. They hired a

husband and wife team, Gail and Ron Syper, to run the day-to-day activity. Gail would be the head waiter and Ron the cook.

Chapter 22

Finally, the restaurant opened with a bang. The place was full, standing room only. Even the bar business seemed to increase. The bowlers from the bar started taking their wives and families to the restaurant.

Skeeter's life was far better than he could have ever hoped for. There was one thing always on his mind - he just couldn't stop thinking of Mary Lou and the kids back in Michigan. What was going on? How were they doing? How were the bills being paid? He couldn't take any chances. He couldn't make contact with anyone. He couldn't send money. He couldn't do anything.

It was five-fifteen. The alarm rang to start the day for Skeeter and Beverly. Skeeter jumped out of bed, clapped his hands, and shouted, "Let's take the day off. Just you and me, babe."

Beverly, startled and somewhat shocked, said, "Have you lost your mind?" They haven't had a day off in weeks.

"No. We will declare it a national holiday. Call down to the restaurant and tell Gail she is in charge. It's Tuesday, a slow day. She can handle it for one day. Make sure she tells Ron. Everything will be OK." He ran over to Beverly, put his arms around her, and started spinning around, "We've earned a day off. We'll pack a lunch and drive to the park. We'll get into The Blue Beauty and go." Skeeter purchased a car two weeks ago. It was an eight-year-old dark blue four-door Ford, now known as The Blue Beauty.

Laughing, Beverly said, "Put me down, you old fool before you kill both of us." Brushing herself off she walked to the phone mumbling under her breath, "He has gone wacko," and called Gail. "Gail, this is Beverly. Palmer has lost his mind. He said we're taking the day off, packing a lunch, and going to the park. He is calling it a national holiday. He said you're in charge. Make sure to tell Ron."

Gail, just as surprised as Beverly about the newfound holiday, responded with, "That sounds great! Don't worry. Everything will be alright. Have fun at the park."

After a couple of cups of coffee and breakfast, Skeeter and Beverly were off to the park in Gibtown. As The Blue Beauty sank into one of the deep potholes, Skeeter said, "Our tax dollars at work."

When Skeeter pulled into the park, the first thing he said was, "Where is the park?" The park was nothing more than a large field that needed mowing. There were two picnic tables that needed painting. And placed between the two picnic tables

was a large garbage barrel that needed emptying. As Skeeter and Beverly got out of the car Skeeter looked up and saw a makeshift baseball field. There were some young boys playing baseball, ranging in age from ten to thirteen.

Looking at the boys playing on the field, Skeeter asked in a surprised voice, “What’s going on with all the kids here?”

“Oh, it must be spring break. Great planning, Palmer.”

The baseball field was a worn-out spot in the grass. The backstop was an old chain link fence that had several holes. The bases were pieces of old rags, the pitcher's mound was a line drawn in the dirt. The boys had one nicked-up bat and a ball that had some of the threads missing.

All of a sudden a fight broke out on the ball field. Skeeter and Beverly had just sat down for their picnic lunch. Skeeter laughed. He got up and walked over to the ball field. When he got there he said, “Guys! Guys!” and started pulling them apart. Soon the boys calmed down.

Skeeter, with a big smile, said, “Are you here to fight or play ball?”

Gary, one of the older boys, said with a Skeeter-type smile, “A little bit of both.”

Skeeter asked the boy, “Who are you?”

The boy replied, “Gary Sappen, my friends call me Cabbage.”

“Why do they call you Cabbage?”

“I don’t know, they just do. What’s your name?”

“William Palmer. My friends call me Palmer.”

“Why do they call you Palmer and not William or Bill?”

"I don't know, they just do." And they all had a good laugh.

Curious, Skeeter asked, "Do you always fight every time you play baseball?"

"Almost. Sometimes we'll have two or three fights."

"Do you like fighting more than playing baseball?"

"No."

"Then why do you fight?"

"Because Jim and a couple of others cheat." The boys started to holler, push, and shove one another again.

With that, Skeeter stepped in to break them up, "OK! OK!" Then he turned back to Gary and asked, "What do you mean 'they cheat'?"

"The catcher calls the balls and strikes. When Jim's the catcher, he calls everything strikes when they should be balls."

"Why would they do that?"

"Because the catcher is the next batter." Skeeter looked confused. So Gary went on to explain, "This is scrub baseball. We don't have enough players for two teams, so we have to rotate positions and batting order. After the first batter is out the catcher gets to bat next."

"Where's your coach?"

"What coach? This is scrub baseball!" All the boys broke out in a laugh.

"You don't have a coach? You don't play in Little League?"

The boys started laughing again.

Gary and his friends knew where they lived. He knew there were the haves and the have-nots, and they were the have-

nots. “That’s for the Main Town boys. They have coaches, dugouts, real bases, lined fields, shirts with sponsors' names on ’em. Nice bats and baseballs. They have everything.” All the boys just nodded. They all knew what Gary said was true. “We have nothing.” The Skeeter type smile was long gone, looking into the eyes of Skeeter he said, “Because we’re the Gibtown boys.”

Skeeter remembered when he was a kid back in Byron, Michigan. They had a pretty good summer baseball program. There were over a hundred and fifty kids that took part. They came from the village and surrounding farms. Though it was a small poor community they still managed to have a quality Little League.

“Why don’t you umpire for us so we can have a fair game and not fight?” The kids nodded.

“Yeah, okay, for a little while.” Skeeter thought to himself *I’m not going to ump from behind the catcher. He only catches about one in five.* Skeeter said, “I’ll ump behind the pitcher so that way I can call the bases too.”

Meanwhile, Beverly walked over and stood behind the backstop. She watched and listened to what was going on.

For two or three innings Skeeter called strikes, balls, and bases as well. Finally, he said, “I’ve had enough, boys, have to go home.”

Gary, who was clearly the leader of the boys, asked, “Are you gonna come back tomorrow?”

Skeeter answered, “Probably not. Have to work, you know.”

Gary informed him, “We’re here around eleven.” Gary noticed Beverly behind the backstop. Beverly was dressed in tight-fitting jeans, a button-down blouse buttoned a little too low and tied at the waist enhancing her figure and revealing a small patch of skin. Her long red hair was tied back in a ponytail. “Is that your wife?”

“No. She's my friend.”

“I bet! She's a knockout. What do you call her?”

“I call her beautiful. You guys can call her Beverly. You better be a gentleman around her. She is a lady.”

With his eyes on Beverly, Gary said, “She sure is.”

Skeeter and Beverly picked up their picnic lunch, got in the car, and started back home.

“It’s not right that these boys don’t have the same equipment that they do in Main Town,” Skeeter reflected.

With a sigh, Beverly replied, “That's the way it is. When the ball-bearing factory closed up most of the people in town lost their jobs but chose to stay. Gibtown has struggled, and so have its children. The grade school is old and rundown. The heating is poor, and in general, it doesn’t get the same maintenance as Main Town schools get. The only thing that Gibtown and Main Town have in common is taxes but without the equal benefits.”

Gibtown was a town within a town and was located on the west side of Gibsonton. Five thousand or so live there. Gibtown was considered the other side of the tracks. The people were less prosperous, less educated than main street Gibsonton.

When they arrived at the apartment, Skeeter said to Beverly, “You go on up, I’m going to see Doc for a minute.”

“Really? You're not going to work, are you?”

"No. I just want to see him for a minute."

Beverly left for the apartment and Skeeter met up with Doc in the bar. Doc was busy as usual in the kitchen as Palmer entered.

"Have a good time on your picnic?"

"Sure, fine. Hey, Doc, got a minute?"

Doc stopped his work, "Sure, what's on your mind?"

"Beverly and I were just at the park. While we were there I noticed a group of boys playing baseball. I went over and started talking to them. What I found out bothered me. Their ball field was terrible, no equipment, no coach. The kids told me that they're not included in the summer baseball program with the Main Town boys. What's going on? We're part of Gibsonton. Why are we treated differently?"

Doc shrugged his shoulders, "That's the way it is."

"That's what Beverly said. What does that mean? 'That's the way it is'?"

"We're Gibtown, they're Main Town. The rich, the poor, the have and have nots. That's the way it has been and always will be. We don't have the education, the money, or the clout to battle City Hall."

"We pay taxes, don't we?"

That's all we get to do is pay taxes. Nothing else. That's the way it is."

Somewhat irritated, Skeeter said, "Well, it's about time someone did something about it."

Doc laughed, "What are you going to do, storm City Hall?"

"Damn right."

Doc laughed a little harder. “Good luck with that!”

“See you, Doc. I'm going upstairs and plot my strategy for storming City Hall.”

Chapter 23

Skeeter went up the inside stairway to the beautiful apartment he and Beverly had completely remodeled. Before, the apartment was only a small part of the upstairs above the bar. They had knocked down walls adding length and width to the apartment and updated the kitchen, bath, everything. As Skeeter entered Beverly was getting dinner. When she looked up and saw Skeeter she smiled and said, “Want another hot cup of coffee?”

Still irritated by the whole ‘that's the way it is’ attitude, Skeeter answered, “I don’t have time right now. Do you know who the head of Parks and Recreation for Gibsonton is?”

“What do you want to know that for?”

“I’m going to storm City Hall. I’m going to find out why the kids in Gibtown are not treated the same as the kids in Main Town.”

"Good luck with that."

"Are you sure you and Doc aren't related? You both say 'that's the way things are' between Main Town and Gibtown. And 'good luck' with trying to get something done."

"Because that is the way things are. It has always been that way."

Looking around the apartment Skeeter said, "It's about to change. Where's the phone book? Oh! Here it is." Turning several pages he found what he was looking for, "Aha! Here it is. Office of Parks and Recreation." Skeeter dialed the number.

A nasal voice answered, "Gibsonton's City Offices, how may I direct your call?"

"I would like to talk to the Director of Parks and Recreation."

"That would be Mr. Wood. Hold, please. I will connect you with his secretary."

A moment later Skeeter heard, "This is Parks and Recreation."

"I would like to speak with Mr. Wood."

"I'm sorry, Mr. Wood is very busy right now. Could someone else help you?"

"No. I need to speak to Mr. Wood in person. If not today, maybe tomorrow, but sometime soon, whenever it would be convenient for Mr. Wood." Skeeter was agitated by the bureaucratic brush-off. "How about if I come tomorrow when you open? I will just wait for him."

She realized that Skeeter was not going to take no for an answer. "What did you say your name was?"

"I am Palmer, William Palmer. I am calling about sponsoring some summer baseball teams."

Wood's secretary thought *Sponsoring a baseball team? Wood is always looking for money to pay for summer baseball.* As she looked at the schedule she said, "Let me see where I can work you in. How about tomorrow, Thursday eight-thirty, before the day gets busy?"

"That sounds great. See you tomorrow at eight-thirty sharp."

At four forty-five, Mr. Harley Wood, director of Gibsonton's Parks and Recreation, buzzed his secretary on the intercom.

"Yes, Mr. Wood."

"What do we have lined up for tomorrow?" he asked.

"Let me see. Oh, yes, first thing, at eight-thirty you have a Mr. Palmer, William Palmer."

Wood interrupted, "I think I know William Palmer."

"He said he wanted to see you about sponsoring some baseball teams," she said in a knowing tone, letting the boss know how keenly aware she was of the needs of Parks and Recreation. "I know you are always looking for sponsors for summer baseball."

About the same time but miles away, while Director Wood was trying to figure out who William Palmer was Skeeter and Beverly were talking about his visit to City Hall.

"You have an appointment with the head of Parks and Recreation? I'm impressed."

"Yep. Tomorrow at eight-thirty."

Beverly, blinking her eyes, said, "Pray tell, Mr. Palmer, what are you going to demand from Mr. Wood?"

"I'm not going to demand anything. I'm going to convince him that the boys in Gibtown deserve the same treatment that the boys have in Main Town."

"Good luck with that."

"You and Doc have to quit saying and thinking things like 'Good luck with that' or that since we live in Gibtown we shouldn't expect the same as in Main Town."

The next morning Skeeter was up at seven and showered. After breakfast, he was out the door, into the car, and down Yellow Brick Road, really Main Street. Then on to City Hall, up to the second floor, to the Office of Parks and Recreation, and over to the receptionist's desk. It was eight-fifteen.

"Hello, my name is Palmer, William Palmer. I have an appointment to see Mr. Wood at eight-thirty."

"Have a seat, Mr. Palmer. Mr. Wood will be with you shortly."

Skeeter sat down in the waiting area. A few minutes later the receptionist buzzed Mr. Wood's secretary. "There is a Mr. Palmer here to see Mr. Wood."

"Send him in," the secretary answered.

The receptionist addressed Skeeter pointing toward a door, "Mr. Palmer, go through that door and Mr. Wood's secretary will help you." The sign on the door read Mr. Harley Wood, Director of Parks and Recreation.

Skeeter stood up quickly, said thanks, and opened the door. He was thinking *So far so good.* As he entered the room,

Wood's secretary pointed and said, "Have a seat. I will let Mr. Wood know you're here."

The secretary called Mr. Wood and said, "Mr. Palmer is here." A moment later, pointing at still another door that had the name Harley Wood, the secretary said, "You can go in now."

Skeeter opened the door and walked to the man standing behind a large mahogany desk with his hand outstretched to greet Mr. William Palmer. Skeeter was getting a little nervous now. His head was starting to spin. Go here, sit there. Go through this door, go through that door. Mr. This, Mr. That. This guy is protected by more doors and people than the President of the United States.

Skeeter shook hands with Wood then motioned for Skeeter to have a seat.

Palmer sat down on a plush green leather chair. Looking around the room Skeeter saw a matching chair and a small sofa. Skeeter had no idea what salary the city of Gibsonton was paying Wood, but they sure didn't hold back the bucks on his office. After both men were seated, Wood said, "My name is Harley Wood, Director of Gibsonton's Parks and Recreation. Please call me Harley."

Skeeter thought *You don't say? Your name is plastered on every door in the place. There is even a mahogany and brass nameplate on your desk!*

Skeeter was very nervous by this time. He had never had to make a presentation to any government official or for that matter to anyone. With a dry mouth, he managed to say, "Nice to meet you. My name is William Palmer. My friends call me Palmer."

Wood was a pleasant-looking man, in his mid to late thirties with light brown hair and a solid build. With a disingenuous smile, Wood asked, "What can I do for you, Mr. Palmer, I mean Palmer? My secretary, Sarah, mentioned that you wanted to sponsor some baseball teams. Is that right?"

Skeeter, stammering, trying to find the right words, "Yes, I mean no, well, probably." Come on Skeeter, grab hold of yourself. "What I mean is, I would like to know why the boys in Gibtown are not treated the same as the boys in Main Town."

The huge smile on Wood's face turned into a more inquisitive look. "I don't know what you mean."

Skeeter went from nervous to anger in a split second. His face flushed as he leaned forward in his chair and thought *You know damn well what I mean*, " but said, "You do know what I mean. What you need to do is take a trip to Gibtown and look at the park and baseball field. There aren't any. The boys use worn-out rugs for bases. Their equipment is broken. Let's not be coy with each other. I'll tell you what I want. I want everything. I want better conditions for the boys in Gibtown. There are no dugouts, proper fields, there isn't anything that resembles a baseball field. I also want the boys from Gibtown to be included in the summer baseball program with the Main Town boys. The Gibtown Business Association will pay the same membership fee as the Main Town sponsors." Of course, there was no such thing. There were no sponsors, no money for equipment. Nothing. No one in Gibtown even knew Skeeter was making this pitch. He had worked himself into a frenzy. "We will buy the same quality shirts and ball caps as the Main boys wear. We will pay for all the equipment and any other expenses

there may be. We would like to sponsor three teams. One team for the nine to ten-year-olds, another for the eleven to twelve-year-olds, and a third for the thirteen to fourteen-year-olds."

Wood sat back in his plush leather chair somewhat startled. He didn't see this coming. When Skeeter finished his presentation Wood relaxed and smiled and said, "You're right."

You could have knocked Skeeter over with a feather. He thought Wood would call for security and have him thrown out. He repeated, "You're right, Mr. Palmer. I can put them on the schedule without any trouble, but to get the fields and dugouts you'll have to take that up with the City Council."

Wood buzzed Sarah.

"Yes, Mr. Wood."

"Sarah, I would like you to remind me to put three teams from Gibtown on our summer baseball schedule." There was a slight pause.

"In what age groups? What -"

Wood interrupted and said, "I will let you know the details when we meet tomorrow to go over the schedule. Thanks, Sarah."

Wood turned toward Skeeter, stuck out his hand and with a genuine smile this time, and said, "How's that?"

Skeeter stood up and shook hands with Wood, but before he could say anything. Wood went on, "Are you the Palmer of Palmer's Place in Gibtown?"

"Yes, I am."

"My wife and I have been thinking of going to your place for some time."

"Come on in, bring a friend. I'm there almost every night. The drinks will be on me."

Chapter 24

KIND WOMAN, tell pitiful story

Skeeter left Wood's office and returned to Palmer's Place. He immediately found Beverly and she excitedly asked, "Well, what happened with Parks and Recreation?"

Skeeter was just as excited and shouted, "We're in! Come on, we have to go tell Doc." He grabbed Beverly's hand, almost lifting her off the floor, and literally ran to the kitchen of Doc's Bar. Doc was working as usual. Skeeter and Beverly almost knocked him over. Skeeter, out of breath, started telling Doc about his experience with Wood.

"Now what we have to do is call a meeting of the Gibtown Business Association and -".

Almost at the same time, Doc and Beverly said, "The *what*?"

"The Gibtown Business Association. We need to buy shirts, equipment, and balls. We need to raise the money to pay the entrance fee. We -"

Doc, shaking his head, said, "There you go again with that 'we' business. Every time you say 'we' it costs me money. What's this business association or whatever you mentioned?"

"Oh, the Gibtown Business Association. We need to call all the business owners in Gibtown to discuss not only the baseball program but the future of Gibtown."

"You know, Palmer, I believe you've bitten off more than you can chew this time," Doc said quite seriously.

"Not really, Doc. Beverly and I will make the calls. We'll meet. Let's see, today is Thursday, next week on Tuesday, say at nine a.m. That's a slow day and time for most of us." Then addressing Beverly, Skeeter continued, "Beverly, when you make your calls tell them we will meet at our restaurant. Tell them the time and place. Tell them that it is important. And tell them there will be free coffee and doughnuts."

She said, "Free coffee and doughnuts, that will get them to come if nothing else does. What should I tell them if they ask what's so important?"

"Tell them if they come, they will know."

Between Thursday and the following Tuesday, Skeeter and Beverly made a lot of phone calls. Many people stopped by the restaurant to ask what was up and inquired about the meeting. All Skeeter and Beverly would say was "Show up and you'll know."

At nine A.M. Tuesday the first meeting of the Gibtown Business Association was about to start. Most of the business

owners in Gibtown were present. Sixteen businesses were represented.

Skeeter tapped on the side of his cup of coffee. "Can I get your attention, please? Has everyone got a cup of coffee and a doughnut? Okay. As you may have heard through the grapevine, I have been working on getting a summer baseball program for the kids here in Gibtown. I will get more into that later. This meeting is more than that. Gibtown has been pushed aside and overlooked for too long by the City Council of Gibsonton." Everyone applauded and hooted. "We need to organize and start looking like a group of businesspeople." More applause. "I have been talking with Doc and Beverly. We would like to know what you think."

Someone shouted out, "Will you have free coffee and doughnuts?"

Skeeter mumbled, "I think I've created a monster," then to the crowd said, "Yes, free coffee and doughnuts." Skeeter was a bit nervous. He had never done anything like this before and didn't know if it would fly or not. He started right in, "We need three sponsors for the Little League Baseball teams from Gibtown. Palmer's Place will sponsor one. Doc said he would sponsor one. Anyone else?"

Hands flew up all over the place and you could hear, "Me" and "I will," from around the room.

"Wow! I didn't think we would have so many offers. Tom, from the Hardware store, you take one." Some of the other merchants started mumbling and calling out, "Some of us others would like to take part too!"

"There are plenty of opportunities to go around. Gibsonton's Park and Recreation maintains four baseball fields. On the outfield fence, from left field to right field, there are small billboard signs advertising businesses from Main Town. Not one of the signs is from Gibtown. I'm sure we could get a couple for us. All season long dozens of games will be played with hundreds of people seeing your ads. I don't think the cost would be any more than the cost of sponsoring a team." Again applause and shouts. The business owners of Gibtown were all in. Several were saying things like, "Sign me up!" and "When do you need my ad?"

When things quieted a bit, Skeeter continued, "We will talk more about it at the next meeting. We would like to set up another meeting two weeks from today, Tuesday at nine A.M. sharp. Anyone wanting to coach a team or help coach one stay after the meeting for a while. We need at least two coaches per team. We will have three teams. You don't have to be a great player, just willing to help." Skeeter wrapped the meeting up quickly so the business owners could get to their businesses. Spirits were high as they grabbed one last doughnut as they went out the door.

Ten guys stayed. "You all want to help coach?"

They all said, "Yes!"

"I need to know what kind of background you have. Little league, high school, that sort of thing. Let's start with you, Kyle." Kyle was an athletic-looking thirty-something man who owned a body shop.

"I played football and baseball. Two years on the varsity in both. I would like to help coach the nine-year-old boys. I have a boy that age."

"I will take the thirteen and fourteen-year-olds," Skeeter stated, "I need one more coach for the eleven and twelve-year-olds."

Kevin, also in his thirties, was Gibtown's handyman. He offered, "I'll take the eleven and twelve-year-olds. I played a lot of baseball when I was a kid."

After all the men were matched to an age group, Skeeter said, "The season doesn't start for another four or five weeks. That sounds like a long time but it's not. We need to get the word out to the community, buy shirts and equipment, and have practice. We will need to meet at least once a week. If you have questions, give me a call."

One week later all the coaches met. Signs had been posted in businesses in Gibtown. Permission slips were handed out at the Gibtown K-8 school letting the boys and their parents know the day, time, and place to sign up and meet their coaches.

Two weeks later the business people of Gibtown met.

Skeeter tapped on his coffee cup to bring the second meeting to order. "Just to let you all know, the coaches met last week. The boys turned in their permission slips. We know which team and coach each boy will play for. We have ordered the shirts with the names of the sponsors on them. The teams have all practiced at least once. The boys chose the name of their teams. Tigers, Bears. Whatever. My team of thirteen and fourteen-year-olds chose Rats. The Gibtown Rats." Wouldn't you know, that's the age group that Gary aka Cabbage was in.

Tom, from the hardware, said, "Palmer, you need something to bang on besides that cup of coffee when you call us to order."

Skeeter went on, "Maybe the next thing we should do is organize. I have given this a lot of thought. We should incorporate. Make it official. Give us a name. Elect officers. Go the whole nine yards."

Someone said, "What's the matter with the Gibtown Business Association?"

"Okay. Any other suggestions?" No one raised a hand. "All in favor of the Gibtown Business Association raise your right hand." Everyone raised their right hand. "Opposed. None. Motion carried." Skeeter fell right into leading the group through a vote. "Now we need to vote for officers. Beverly has been keeping notes acting as sort of a secretary. That doesn't mean she needs to continue. I would like to take nominations from the floor first for president, then vice president, secretary, and treasurer. Do I hear a nomination for president?"

Although Skeeter had led the group, he was completely out of his element. They all started to laugh. Someone said, "That's you, Palmer." Bill from the bakery stood up and said, "I nominate Palmer for President and Beverly for secretary."

Another person stood up and said, "Make Doc VP."

Still another person stood and said, "I nominate Cary Volt for Treasurer, he is an accountant and works at the Gibsonton Community Bank in Gibtown."

Someone in the crowd said, "All in favor say 'yea'." There were laughs and shouts of 'yea' around the room.

Another voice called out, "Good! The motion passed!" And more laughter erupted. Skeeter wasn't sure what the correct protocol was but knew this wasn't it. He said, "I don't think it's done that way."

Sherri Peterson, one of the few women business owners in Gibtown and owner of the Gibtown Independent, said, "Let's start over and let someone nominate a slate of officers. Palmer for president, Doc VP, Cary Treasurer, and Beverly Secretary. Then ask 'Is there any other nomination?' If there isn't any, then ask 'All in favor of the slate of nominees raise your right hand'. That's it." She sat down. No one said a word for a moment.

Skeeter, thoroughly stunned, turned to Beverly, "Did you get that down?"

"Yes, Palmer, there is a motion to elect the slate of officers made by Sherri Peterson."

With a closer semblance to proper procedure in place, Skeeter went on, "Do we have a second to the motion?" Someone seconded the motion. "All in favor raise your right hand." Everyone raised their right hand. "Any objections?" There were no objections. "Motion passed."

Chapter 25

FOOD HERE
if you WORK

OR

At the May first meeting of the Gibtown Business Association, someone suggested that they should have their own Memorial Day celebration. Skeeter said, "We don't want to separate ourselves from Main Town anymore than we already are. Maybe we can enter a float representing Gibtown. If you want I will look into the matter."

Everyone thought that was a good idea. A Memorial Day float committee was formed consisting of Sherri Peterson, Beverly, and Mary Curt from the flower store.

The next day Skeeter phoned the Gibsonton Chamber of Commerce, they were the people in charge of the Memorial Day parade.

"Good morning, Gibsonton Chamber of Commerce. This is Jennifer, how may I help you?"

"My name is Skeeter," he realized what he had just said and quickly corrected, "Palmer, William Palmer from Gibtown."

Jennifer wondered if he just said *Skeeter* but quickly went on, "May I ask what your concern is?"

I would like to meet with the person that is in charge of the floats for the Memorial Day parade."

"That would be Pat Garfield."

"I would like to arrange for a meeting with Ms. Garfield today if that is possible?"

"How about eleven o'clock today?"

"Thanks. That would be great."

At eleven o'clock Skeeter entered the Chamber of Commerce office. He approached the receptionist's desk and said, "Good morning, I am William Palmer, I have an eleven o'clock with Ms. Garfield."

"Yes, Mr. Palmer. Please have a seat over there," she said pointing to several seats in the lobby.

Jennifer rang Pat Garfield, still wondering what she heard earlier from Skeeter. Ms. Garfield, there is a Mr," with a slight pause, "Palmer, a Mr. William Palmer from Gibtown who would like to speak to you about the Memorial Day parade."

Ms. Garfield questioned herself, *William Palmer... I don't believe I know a William Palmer.* "Yes, Jennifer, send him in."

Jennifer, with a pencil in her hand, pointed to Pat Garfield's office door, "Mr. Palmer, Ms. Garfield will see you now."

Skeeter got to his feet, nodded, and said thank you to Jennifer. He walked to the door which had a bronze nameplate, which read *Ms. Patricia Garfield.*

He knocked on the door. A voice said, "Come in."

Skeeter opened the door and walked toward another large mahogany desk. The office was similar to the Director of Parks and Recreation, Harley Wood's office. Instead of green chairs and sofa, they were red.

Ms. Garfield, with a pleasant smile, gestured to Skeeter to have a seat and said, "Mr. Palmer, would you like a cup of coffee or a glass of water?"

Ms. Garfield wore her hair in a bun and a pair of glasses on a jeweled string around her neck that rested on her very large bosom. For a split second, Skeeter thought of what having a cup of coffee meant between him and Beverly. He said, "No, no coffee," a pause, "or water." As he sat down he calculated she'd dress out at three hundred pounds.

He said, "Please just call me Palmer." Collecting his thoughts he got right to the point. "I would like to know if the merchants from Gibtown could enter a float in the Memorial Day Parade."

After a slight pause, she said, "I don't see why not. I will send you a copy of the regulations on what materials can and cannot be used, the size of the float, length, width, height, and so on. The regulations aren't that much. But there are state and local fire laws we have to abide by. If you have any questions, give me a call. I am looking forward to working with you." She went on to say, "You know, this parade is a big deal here in Gibsonton. There will be school bands, tractors, kids riding

bicycles decorated with crepe paper, Masons driving little cars, floats from the many different clubs, horses, and a carnival." Skeeter went numb. *Carnival.* Skeeter stood, shook hands with Pat, and said thank you.

As he left the building Skeeter thought *What a nice and pleasant lady Ms. Garfield was.*

She mentioned a carnival.

Could it be Dobbs' carnival? Probably not because he is in the north country this time of year. However, there could be someone at this carnival that he knew from his time working at Dobbs'. Carny people move from one carnival to another all the time.

Skeeter thought *No problem. We will go to the parade and not go to the carnival. Easier said than done. Beverly will want to go to the carnival. I'll have to run the risk of someone recognizing me. What will I say to her? "Oh, by the way, Beverly, there is this matter of me assuming my friend Palmer's identity when he died because I killed three people back in Michigan. Then of course there's the mob." I will just have to go and chance it. Ride a couple of rides, eat some popcorn and cotton candy. And wham bam, thank you, ma'am, we're out of there.*

Skeeter and Beverly went to the parade and the carnival. They rode a few rides and had some popcorn and cotton candy. All went well, as he'd hoped. Skeeter kept a close eye out for anyone he might have known from his carnival days. Perfect. He did not recognize anyone.

The Gibtown Business Association did enter a float and won third place out of twenty-three entries.

Over the next few weeks baseball season started and ended. The boys from Gibtown did quite well. They didn't win as many as they lost but had a good time. There were only a few instances where a curse word was thrown out and only a couple of minor fights but all in all a good season.

A big end-of-season picnic and carnival were given by Gibsonton's Parks and Recreation. Skeeter kept wondering *What is it with all these carnivals? Will Dobbs show up this time?* It was still the time of the year when Dobbs should be north. Again, Skeeter dodged the bullet.

It was late August and time for football. The Gibtown Business Association sponsored two Little League Football teams. Football was right up the alley for the boys from Gibtown. You could hit, bite, scratch, spit, swear, and for the most part get away with it. Although the boys enjoyed football more than baseball they still didn't win as many games as they lost. After football would be basketball. Basketball was not going to be nearly as much fun for the Gibtown boys. You touch someone in basketball you get a penalty. They would become the most penalized team in their league. What was good about the basketball season was that for the first time the K-8 Gibtown school would not have to be part of a Main Town school team, they would play as a team of their own.

Life was going extremely well for Skeeter. He had a wonderful significant other in Beverly and a great friend in Doc. Skeeter felt as close to Doc as he had toward Palmer. His

restaurant business was a huge success and was about to become even better.

Chapter 26

While being the president of the Gibtown Business Association, running little baseball, football, and basketball programs, Skeeter still had to run the restaurant business.

During one of the few lulls in Skeeter's life, he had a conversation with Beverly and Doc. “I was thinking. The restaurant is doing pretty well, but I think we should add something more. We need to add a buffet and more items to the menu. We will need to add more tables. We need to advertise in *Gibsonton’s News* and in the *Gibtown Independent,* and WREV TV.”

Doc replied, “There you go again with that ‘we’ business. You know, Palmer, that sounds like a big undertaking but I think you might be right.”

“Me too,” Beverly chimed in.

"That scares me when the both of you agree with me so quickly."

"Give us an overall plan. You do have one, don't you?" Beverly asked.

With great confidence, Skeeter said, "I have been thinking about this for some time. I have quite a detailed plan. First, let me lay out the menu. We will keep the same menu we've always had for the first three days of the week. Monday, Tuesday, and Wednesday. The other four nights of the week we will switch to buffet style but with a classy twist, which I'll explain in a minute.

"On Fridays, we will have seafood. Not just fish and chips. Real seafood. Clams, shrimp, lobster, crab legs, and clam chowder. Saturdays will be a more traditional 'Where's the beef?' night. Beef, ham, and chicken. Sundays will be a brunch all day with sausage, bacon, ham, sausage gravy, eggs any way you want them: over easy, sunny side up, including different omelets."

Beverly asked, "What happens on Thursdays?"

"I thought you would never ask. Thursday will be the best of them all. Thursday will be a foul night."

At almost the same time Beverly and Doc said, "Foul night? What's foul night?"

"Foul, you know, birds. We will have a bird menu. Chicken, duck, turkey, pheasant, ostrich. Maybe more."

Doc, always thinking of the business angle, said, "Sounds quite expensive to me.

"I believe people will drive fifty miles or more just to eat here." Returning to his plan, Skeeter went on, "Now let me tell

you about the layout of the restaurant. We have plenty of room right now for forty people. I would like to add three more tables of four to bring the total capacity to fifty-two. There will be room for a soup and salad bar that will not be used Monday through Wednesday and concealed by a curtain when not used.

"Now let me explain about Thursday through Sunday. Our buffet will not be typical where the customers get seated, walk to the buffet bar, pick up a plate and serve themselves their meat, walk to another area for vegetables, another area for salad, soup, and so on. To make our buffet special, tables will have white table cloths covered by a glass top to make it easy to clean but will look very nice. Each table will have a lighted candle. To add atmosphere, the customer will be met at the door by me. I will be dressed like Humphrey Bogart's character Rick Blaine in *Casablanca*. Bogie wore a white sports coat, black bow tie, black dress pants, and black shoes. His nightclub was called *Rick's Americana*. The wait staff will all wear the same attire, men and women: a white long sleeve shirt, black bow tie, black cummerbund, black dress pants, and black shoes. I will escort the party to their table and give each person their own individual menu specific for that night. There will be separate wine and beverage menus.

"Instead of the waiter taking the order and writing it down, customers will fill out the checklist and give it to the waiter after making their selections. At the top of each menu, *Palmer's Place* will be printed. There will also be ballpoint pens at every table with the name *Palmer's Place* on them. The menu will be a checklist of entrees offered for that night. Each customer will be given a glass of water and asked if there are any

questions. If not, the wait staff will leave and come back to pick up their order.

"When the wait staff returns he or she will take the menus back to the kitchen and the beverage orders to the bar. Meanwhile, the customers will go to the salad bar and get their other food items such as vegetables, salad, and soup. After their first order, each customer will be given a new checklist menu. They can order as many entrees as they want and go to the salad bar as many times as they want, just like any other buffet.

"The average cost per food order depends on the night. On Friday, seafood night, it will be twelve ninety-five, if a person wants lobster that would be sixteen ninety-five, or more depending on market price. On Saturday, 'Where's the beef?' night, it will cost eleven ninety-five. Sunday brunch, ten ninety-five, and our special foul night, fourteen ninety-five." Skeeter wrapped up his explanation and looked at Doc and Beverly. "What do you think?"

Doc and Beverly were dumbfounded. They simply could not believe how well thought out Skeeter's plans for the new buffet were. Everything down to do the tablecloth and lighted candles on the table. They both looked at each other and said, "Sure, why not?"

Skeeter's plan was immediately put into action. Three tables and a dessert bar were added. New menus were printed up. New vendors were contacted. Every penny that Palmer had and a big loan from Doc went into the new restaurant.

Skeeter went all out in advertising. He put ads in the *Gibsonton News*, *Gibtown Independent,* plus three or four other

newspapers from surrounding towns, including radio and even television.

As the saying goes "build it and they will come". And come, they did! Rich people, and not so rich, politicians, and the average Joe. It was standing room only. Palmer's Place served fifty-two guests every half hour from four until seven-thirty P.M. Four hundred guests a night, four nights a week. At least fifteen hundred a week times thirteen dollars a plate. You do the math. It was a lot of money.

Skeeter was at the top. He loved playing Humphrey Bogart and he did a great job. He greeted everyone. His great smile paid off. He was one of the best-known people in Gibsonton City, Hillsborough County, and the surrounding area.

Chapter 27

At the October meeting of the Gibtown Business Association, Ryan Aaron, owner-operator of the local IGA grocery store, mentioned that it was an election year. Everything from the President of the United States to Gibsonton's city council was up for election. Ryan said, "What we need is to run someone from Gibtown for the council." Someone else said, "We haven't had a person on the city council ever." Then everyone started talking at once. One person hollered, "That's why our roads are so bad!" Another shouted, "Yeah, and there's poor street lighting!" Still, another added, "There are no real parks for our kids!"

Skeeter questioned, "Well, who do you think we should nominate?"

Everyone was smiling and said in unison, "YOU!" Just as if they planned the whole thing. Which they had. The

businessmen and women of Gibtown knew this was their chance to get respect from Gibsonton's government. They had been taxed without representation long enough. Beverly and Doc were part of the plot to run Skeeter for city councilman.

"Look, I'm no politician," Skeeter pleaded. He was feeling unqualified and anxious.

Luke the barber offered, "Everyone in Gibtown will vote for you."

"Even if they did, that would only be a small portion of Gibsonton's total city population," Skeeter tried again.

Cary Volt, the local banker and accountant, said, "We looked into that. Here is what we found out. There are three open seats to be filled. Two will more than likely be filled by two people already on the council from Gibsonton, leaving one open seat. We know that two additional people from Main Town have filled out forms to be placed on the November ballot. That would give voters in Main Town two of their own to vote for, plus you. We should wait for the last day to file, which will be in nine days. That way we won't tip our hand and let them know we're trying to split their vote with you coming from out of nowhere for the win. Of course, most of Main Town voters will vote for Main Town candidates. However, some, no, a lot will vote for you. You're well known now. All of Gibtown will vote for you."

Someone yelled out, "We may vote two or three times!"

Cary continued, "This plan can work for you, Palmer."

Everyone started gathering around Skeeter. "Come on Palmer. What do we have to lose?"

Skeeter, not too enthusiastically, said, "OK."

Cary whispered to Skeeter, "You are a registered voter, aren't you?"

"I don't think so."

Cary instructed Skeeter quietly, "Go down tomorrow and register." Then turning to the crowd, "We need to appoint a committee to elect C. William Palmer to the Gibsonton City Council." Everyone went crazy.

But Skeeter had questions that needed to be clarified. The crowd settled as Skeeter asked, "Aren't there districts, or wards, or something like that you have to run in?" Skeeter knew in larger cities there were, but had little knowledge of the political system.

Cary answered, "No, elected positions are on an at-large basis. Whoever gets the most votes wins. If there are three openings and four people run, the three with the most votes win. The more people from Main Town that enter the election the more Main Town votes will be spread among them. Everyone in Gibtown will vote for you. You stand a good chance."

Skeeter asked, still looking for a way out, "What is the percentage of Gibtown voters to Main Town?"

"About twenty-five percent. It will be close, but you're going to get more Main Town votes than you think." Volt outlined the campaign. He was named campaign chairman to the committee to elect C. William Palmer to the Gibsonton City Council. Sherri Peterson, owner of the print shop and weekly newspaper the *Independent*, had already made rough drafts of leaflets and small yard signs promoting C. William Palmer. Cary announced, "We will meet here tomorrow at nine a.m. and go over our plan of attack."

Cary looked at Palmer, "You're going to win, Palmer."

The next day Skeeter registered to vote. No questions, no big deal. Nine days later, the last day that a person could make an application to run for Gibsonton City Council, Skeeter entered City Hall, walked to the reception counter, and asked, "Could I have the forms needed to run for city council?" The lady at the counter almost fell over.

"Why sure, Mr. Palmer. Just a moment." She went over to a table and returned. "Here they are. Only one page. You can fill them out right over there," pointing to a table. "Just bring them back to me so I can put the stamp of the city and date on them. You're just in time. We close in fifty-five minutes."

Skeeter said, "Thank you," and walked to the table. He filled out the form and returned to the counter. The lady stamped the forms. She made a copy for Skeeter and said with a smile, "There's your copy, Mr. Palmer." Then looking at the clock added, "Just in time, you had nineteen minutes left. And by the way, Mr. Palmer, good luck."

With that, Skeeter replied, "Thanks. Make sure to vote for me."

Skeeter returned to the restaurant where Beverly, Doc, and Cary (and of course Paul and Tim) were waiting. He walked in smiling, waving the copy of the application to seek office. "So far so good," Skeeter declared. Everyone cheered.

The following day at nine A.M. sharp the "Elect Palmer for city council" committee met at Palmer's Place. Once everyone was seated Cary said, "We will move to the break

room in the back of the restaurant. That will be our war room from now on. All meetings and materials will be there."

The war room as Cary called it, was not a very large area, but it made do. "There will be phones installed and a few other necessities to run a campaign for city council. Sherri and Tom will be passing out copies of the proposed handouts, bumper stickers, and yard signs. As you can see, the handouts are tri-fold and in color. Sherri did an outstanding job. There will be teams of two people each, which will have designated areas of the city that they will be responsible for. We will cover the entire city of Gibsonton. Knock on every door and hand out leaflets to every house asking if we can put up a "Vote for Palmer" yard sign. Make sure you tell the residence at each place that you will put up and take down the sign. Some of you will be in charge of the business district. Go to every business. Ask if you can place a small stack of leaflets and a sign in their window. If you belong to a service organization such as Lions Club, Kiwanis Club even if you do not belong to the one in Gibsonton, and ask if Palmer can speak at one of their meetings. Allan Mallory and I will see that Palmer is invited to the panel discussions such as "Meet the Candidate" where all candidates get a chance to speak. We will also have a few radio and TV ads."

In a serious voice, Skeeter said, "That sounds quite expensive."

Cary affirmed, "Palmer, it will be. If you want to win and have someone from Gibtown on the council, you will have to pay." He went on, "So everyone here, break out your checkbooks! Whatever you feel you can contribute, add another hundred dollars to it!"

The one thing the Gibtown Business Association didn't lack was energy. They covered the entire city, every house, every business. Skeeter spoke to any group that would have him. He did an excellent job. He was very nervous at the beginning, but as time wore on Skeeter was a real campaigner with his abundance of energy and his great smile. Skeeter was seen every day and night walking the main streets and side streets of Gibsonton handing out leaflets and talking with people. No other candidate was as visible as Skeeter.

The Palmer campaign workers offered anyone in Gibtown or Main Town a free ride to and from the election polls. The people who didn't have transportation were the people who could identify with Skeeter. They might live in Main Town but they had a Gibtown budget.

Finally, it was Election Day. A bright, sunny day. There was a big turnout at the election polls. It was later reported that it was the largest turnout for an election that Gibtown ever had. A good sign for Skeeter. It was also reported that it was one of the largest turnouts for Main Town. Not so good for Skeeter.

Chapter 28

At seven P.M. Election Day, the polls were closed. A scheduled victory party began at Palmer's Place. Everybody was happy. Cary Volt stepped to the microphone. "Can I have your attention? Palmer would like to say a few words." Someone from the crowd yelled out, "Make it short, Palmer, we've got a lot of drinking to do!" A large burst of laughter and cheers broke out.

"I will keep it short. I would like to thank each and every one of you for your support and hard work. No matter what your part was in my election effort it could not have happened without you. Win or lose, thank you all." The crowd went crazy with cheers.

Cary took the microphone and said, "We are celebrating a victory here tonight!"

The ballot on this November Election Day had many positions and issues. This was a presidential and gubernatorial

election year, with the House of Representatives and senators. This was a huge ballot. All the big races would probably be in by midnight, but the county, city, and school boards would not be counted until noon or later the following day.

Later that evening Skeeter and Beverly retired to their apartment. He went to sleep almost immediately. The party went on until way past midnight.

Skeeter and Beverly were up the next morning at eight-thirty, had breakfast, and were in the war room by nine-fifteen.

Cary and two or three others were already there.
Skeeter looked at Cary and said, “What's up?”

Cary said, “I called down to the county offices and talked to Fran Morrison, chairperson for the county board of elections. She said that Ken Offener was elected mayor, Mary Carson elected treasurer, Charlene May elected secretary.”

“Wow! What a news flash,” Skeeter said sarcastically. They were all unopposed. Everyone had a good laugh.

Cary went on, “Fran said they wouldn’t have news on the three council seats before noon.”

Skeeter said, “Ladies and gentlemen, I have a restaurant to run. I better get to it.” The others in the war room agreed they had places to be and they all left. On the way out Cary said, “Meet you back here around one.”

At one o’clock Cary and the others arrived at the restaurant and started walking toward the war room. Cary waved to Skeeter to join them.

Once everyone was in and settled, Cary addressed the small group, “Now that we are here I will call Fran at the county

board of elections." Cary placed the call and put the phone on speaker so everyone in the room could hear the conversation. "Good morning, Hillsborough County Office. How may I direct your call?"

"This is Cary Volt. I would like to speak to Mrs. Morrison."

"Hold please."

Then after a short pause, they heard, "Good morning, Cary, this is Fran. There still isn't much I can tell you about the three council seats. It's looking pretty good for William and Jay, the two incumbents, as for the third seat, it is just too close to call. What I think we're going to do is make the announcement on the six o'clock news. We should have an answer by then. I would suggest that you stay tuned to your TV and watch the news. Sorry I can't give you any more than that."

"Thanks, Fran." He hung up the phone. "I guess they want to make a real production out of it. Let's get the word out and meet at Doc's Bar at five-thirty. He has big-screen TVs."

At five forty-five Cary Volt entered Doc's Bar and Grill. There was standing room only. At five-fifty Cary stood on a chair and said, "Alright everyone, let's be quiet so we can see and hear the TVs." There were two televisions in the bar. At six o'clock the news intro started. *"This is WREV channel one Gibsonton."*

The announcer said, "Good evening, everyone, I'm Lanny Fox with news from around the city, around the state, and around the world. Tonight's headline is the recent election right here in Gibsonton. More specifically, the three city council seats. With me tonight is Fran Morrison, chairperson of the

Hillsborough County Election Board." The TV screen widened to show both Lanny Fox and Fran Morrison.

"Welcome to WREV News, Fran."

"Thanks for inviting me."

"Let's get right to it. Who are the big winners in the Gibsonton election?"

Fran announced, "The mayor-elect is Ken Offener, the secretary is Charlene May, and the treasurer is Mary Carson. These three were unopposed."

"I have been told that it was one of the closest elections in Gibsonton History."

Fran confirmed, "Yes, that is correct."

"Should we have a drum roll?" Lanny asked lightheartedly. "It is my understanding, Fran, the three candidates with the most votes fill the open seats. Is that right?"

"That's right. The winning candidates could live next door to each other or across town.

"With no further ado, let's have it. Who are the next city council members?"

In a very official voice, Fran announced, "The candidate with the most votes is William Bishop, the candidate with the second most votes is Jay Parks, they are both incumbents. The third candidate with the most votes -"

"Hang on to your seats, history could be made here," Lanny interjected.

"The third person with the most votes is William Palmer!"

Doc's Bar went crazy. Yelling, jumping up and down, slapping each other on the back, beer sprayed all over. Skeeter

was lifted on the shoulders of two men and carried around the bar and out into the street. No one from Gibtown had ever been elected to the city council. It wasn't a victory for Skeeter, it was a victory for Gibtown. Residents left their homes and joined in.

The celebration lasted into the wee hours of the morning.

The next morning the phone rang at Palmer's Place. Gail answered the phone. "Hello, Palmer's." She laid the phone down and called Palmer, "It's for you."

"Who is it?"

"Some dude says he's the mayor."

"What would the mayor call me for?" Then, picking up the phone, Skeeter said, "Hello, this is Palmer."

"Congratulations on your election! This is Ken Offener."

"Thank you, Mayor, it was quite a surprise."

"Not that big a surprise. I was calling not only to congratulate you on your win but also to let you know at the first meeting of the new city council, which is next Monday at seven p.m. at City Hall," as if Palmer was not already aware of the city council meetings, "the first thing I will do is introduce each member of the council. I will then ask each council member to submit which committee they would like to serve on. I will send over a copy of the agenda and a list of the various committees. You will have a week from Monday to submit your choices. I will explain everything at the meeting. I thought I would give you a heads up."

"Thanks, Mayor, I appreciate it."

"When we are not doing official business, just call me Ken".

"Same here, I mean call me Palmer."

At City Hall on the second Monday in November at seven p.m. Mayor Ken Offener called the meeting to order, striking his gavel three times, "Madam Secretary, will you please call the roll?"

One by one the secretary called the names of the Gibsonton City Council. When she came to Palmer she said 'William Palmer'. The city council chambers exploded with cheers. The room was packed full of spectators, most of whom were from Gibtown.

The Mayor hammered his gavel for silence. With a smile, he said, "We haven't had attendance this large in a long time." He went on, "Next on the agenda if there are no objections, I will appoint an oversight committee of three to assign committee members." There were no objections. "The oversight committee will consist of me, Mary Carson, and Carlene May. The reason these three are chosen is that they do not sit on any of the committees. Attached to each council person's agenda is a list of all committees. Take the list home, look it over, and mark it in the box next to those you would like to serve on, and return the list to the City Clerk's office by five p.m. next Monday. You will all be on at least three committees and chair at least one of the three. The rest of the meeting was business as usual.

During the following week, Skeeter filled out his committee wish list which consisted of Parks and Recreation, Streets and Lights, and Budget, and returned it to the City Clerk's office.

At City Hall at the next regular meeting of the Gibsonton City Council was called to order by Mayor Ken Offener. After

the roll call was taken Mayor Offener asked the secretary to read the committee assignments for the next term.

The secretary read each councilperson's assignment. She announced Palmer's last, "Mr. William Palmer: Park and Recreation and Streets and Lights. Mr. Palmer will chair the Hospitality committee." Skeeter was happy that he got two of the three committees that he wanted. Chairing Hospitality wouldn't be all that bad.

On Thursday following the City Council meeting the first meeting of the Park and Recreation Committee met consisting of Robert Parks and William Bishop both of Main Town, and Skeeter. Skeeter made a motion that there should be a plan to build a new baseball facility in Gibtown comparable to those in Main Town. The motion also stated that the park would be maintained on the same schedule as Main Town with regards to mowing and painting of tables. After much discussion, the motion failed two to one. Also, at the meeting was Park and Recreation director Harley Wood who gave his full support to Skeeter. When the motion failed two to one, he was upset but recognized the politics of the situation between two Main Town votes against one Gibtown vote. Palmer realized he would never get anything passed in the committee.

The meeting of the Streets and Light committee consisting of Mary Carson and Charlene May, along with Skeeter didn't go any better. Skeeter made a motion to spend the same amount of money on street construction and street repair in Gibtown as in Main Town. The motion failed two to one. Politics again.

For some time Skeeter had been meeting with Roger Smythe, a builder and general contractor from Gibtown. Roger was fully licensed by the state and county. Skeeter and Roger had been designing a baseball field for Gibtown. Although Skeeter's committee motions were denied he had another plan in mind hoping that the council as a whole would vote in his favor. This would be a do-or-die proposal. His motions would always fail in committee. Gibtown would never reap the benefit of him being their representative.

Following the committee meetings, the next regular City Council met. After the formality of the opening of the council, Mayor Offener asked if there was any new business. Skeeter raised his hand and asked, "Mr. Mayor, may I have the floor?" The mayor wondered what he was up to but granted him permission to speak.

Skeeter was nervous realizing the importance of what he was doing. It was an improper motion he was about to make. He knew that the mayor could call him out of order and his whole proposal and the future of Gibtown's Parks would fail.

Skeeter cleared his throat and forged ahead. He made a motion that the Parks and Recreation Department gather preliminary estimates for the construction of a baseball field in Gibtown and also schedule maintenance on the grounds on a regular basis. Skeeter contended that the taxpayers in Gibtown pay toward parks but have not received any benefits. A huge cheer went up from the Gibtown residents who filled the chambers. Mayor Offener banged his gavel hard and shouted, "Order! Order!"

Skeeter tried again, "If I may continue, I would like to submit a detailed plan to build a baseball field in Gibtown. The plan has detailed blueprints, a cost sheet, and a material list compiled by Mr. Roger Smythe. Mr. Smythe is a fully licensed general contractor by the state and county. I have also had Mr. Wood, director of Parks and Recreation, review these plans." Then turning his attention to the director said, "Mr.
Wood, what is your general appraisal of the plan?"

Mr. Wood answered, "After a careful review I believe the plans are very doable. The cost is far below any that we have spent for comparable baseball fields in Main Town."

Skeeter went on, "The plan I propose will ask the City of Gibsonton to pay for only the material cost of the project. The labor will be provided by the Gibtown Business Association under the direction of Mr. Roger Smythe. The total cost will be forty to fifty percent less than normal."

Another cheer went up from the Gibtown resident attendees.

With a scowl on his face and a hammering of his gavel, the mayor shouted, "Order! Order! Or I will clear the room!"

Skeeter was enraged at the suggestion that his constituents would be removed, "That's right, Mayor, bring in the SWAT team to clear everyone so only your voice can be heard!"

The room calmed down after Skeeter's remarks.

The mayor knew that Palmer's motion failed at the Parks and Recreation committee meeting just days before. He also knew what Skeeter was up to. Looking directly at Skeeter with a look of 'don't push me too far on this' the mayor said, "You

know, Mr. Palmer, this matter should be brought before the Parks and Recreation committee. However, this is what I will do for you and your friends in Gibtown. I will appoint a special committee to review your proposal. This committee will consist of the three-member Parks and Recreation committee, myself, the city manager Mr. Jay Fritz, Chairperson of the Ways and Means committee Mr. Charles Farr, and the director of Parks and Recreation Mr. Wood. Mr. Palmer, you will chair this special committee. The committee will meet weekly at a day and time you choose. The meeting will be held at City Hall in the large meeting room. Does that meet with your approval, Mr. Palmer?" Offener's tone was sarcastic and patronizing.

With a smirk, Skeeter responded with, "It sounds like a plan."

"So be it. The meetings will be closed to the public. Minutes of the special committee will be taken and available for the public," Offener concluded.

Skeeter did not bring up his concerns about the Streets and Lights. One fight at a time.

Over the next several months, the special Parks and Recreation Committee met once a week, sometimes more. By early April the construction of the new baseball field in Gibtown started. While the planning for the parks went on, Skeeter continued his fight for Gibtown equity for better roads. Triple the money was spent on Gibtown streets ending Skeeter's first year on the city council. The future will bring better streets and better parks.

Chapter 29

FREE TELEPHONE

September. It was near the end of Skeeter's second year on the City Council.

Skeeter was not only one of the best known and liked people in Gibtown, but throughout Gibsonton City and Hillsborough County, great things were said about this guy Palmer.

At the close of the September meeting of the Gibtown Business Association, Cary Volt asked Palmer to meet with him and a few others in the War Room in the back of the restaurant.

After Cary and Skeeter arrived, Cary shut the door and said, "Have a seat, Palmer." Also in the room were the ten people who were part of the committee that spearheaded Skeeter's campaign to win his council seat.

"What's up? You all look pretty serious," Skeeter observed.

Doc answered, “It's only two months away from the election.”

Skeeter with a big smile said, “Do you think I am going to have a hard time getting re-elected?”

“We don’t want you to run again. We have someone else in mind,” Doc said in a low tone.

Skeeter was shocked. He said, “Okay, who do you have in mind?”

“Cary Volt.”

Skeeter responded quietly, “You couldn’t have picked a better person.”

Cary said with a smile and clap on the back, “We want you to run for State Representative!” Everyone in the room started laughing. Someone said, “Gotcha, didn’t we!”

Skeeter was dumbfounded. “State Representative? You guys are crazy, it's impossible. Next, you’ll want me to run for governor!”

Agreeing, Doc said, “That will be two or three elections from now!”

Cary added, “It is quite possible. Everything is lining up just like it did when you ran for city council. The Eighty-Seventh District’s State Representative seat is open. No incumbent. Seventy-five percent of the Eighty-Seventh District is Hillsborough County and Gibsonton City. You are one of the most popular people in the district. The one drawback is the Republican Party is the strongest political party in the district right now and they have their candidate. The Democrats are looking for someone. When we mentioned you, they were ecstatic about the idea. It will be a tough campaign and a costly

one. With the money we can raise and the money the Democrats are willing to put in, it should be enough. You have to do it, Palmer. If you don't win you can run for Gibsonton City Council or even Mayor next election. Offener will be ready to step down by then. What do you say?"

Skeeter was smiling broadly, "I still think you're crazy, but I'll do it."

The room exploded in applause and congratulations.

Cary brought the small crowd back to order by banging on the table. All eyes turned to him and he turned to Palmer and went on, "The Democratic Party for the Eighty-Seventh District said they would not run anyone else in the Primary giving you a clear shot in the general election in November which would save a lot of money to be used for the general election." Addressing the room, he said, "The die has been cast. The Gibtown committee that organized the "Palmer for City Council" will spearhead the election for "Palmer for State Representative" assisted by the Eighty-Seventh District Democratic Party. They will arrange speaking engagements, newspaper, radio, and television ads."

When the meeting ended the committee members drifted back to their businesses.

Meanwhile back at the ranch, as one might say, the activity of the Democrats did not go unnoticed by the Republicans. Quite the contrary. The Republican power machine was quite impressed with Gibtown's Mr. Palmer.

Shortly after the meeting in the War Room at Palmer's Place, word leaked out about Palmer's running for State Representative.

The Republican Party of the Eighty-Seventh District was located in downtown Gibsonton. The Republican Party organization was much larger than the Democrats'. In the off-year, they have one full-time staffer. During election time there were several. At this time the Republican Party controlled the state legislature, the governor's seat, most of the local, county, and city governments in Florida.

The chairman for the Eighty-Seventh District for the Republican Party was a man by the name of Jerome Van Buren. Van Buren's ancestors were involved in politics in one form or another for over a hundred years in Gibsonton. His family went back to the Civil War days. Van Buren was a large man nearly six feet tall and close to three hundred pounds. He spoke slowly and chose his words carefully. He looked and sounded like the old-time movie actor Burl Ives. He was more than the head of the Republican Party; he was the boss and everyone called him Boss. He lived in an old but well-maintained plantation-style house on three hundred acres, which had been passed down from generation to generation. Many, many years ago the Van Buren plantation had over a thousand acres that grew mainly cotton and employed several slaves. Now he has forty or fifty Black Angus breeding cows. No one really knew where Jerome Van Burn got his money.

It was a bright Monday morning a few days after the word leaked out about Palmer's candidacy. Jerome "Boss" Van Buren called a meeting of the Eighty-Seventh District Republican Party.

Politics can be a dirty game. The higher the office the dirtier it gets. At the state House of Representatives level, it is pretty dirty. The stakes are high. There is a lot of money floating around. Everyone wants a piece of it.

The Boss was a little nervous. He heard a lot of good things about Palmer. That wasn't good for The Boss. The Eighty-Seventh District seat was open, the incumbent who was one of The Boss's guys moved up. Now the new candidate the Republicans were backing wasn't that strong. It looked like Palmer was by far the stronger of the two.

The Boss shouted, "Billy!" Billy was a little fellow, The Boss's gopher, the guy that could find everything about everybody. His real name was William Lee. Billy was almost the opposite of Jerome Van Buren. Billy was short, just shy of five foot six, a hundred twenty-five pounds soaking wet. He wore square black horn-rim glasses and had a nasal sound to his voice; he was devoted to The Boss.

"I want to know who this Palmer guy is. I want to know all about him. He didn't just fall out of the sky. He has a past. He has a history. Everybody has a closet and every closet has at least one skeleton. I want to know what the skeleton is and I want to rattle it hard. You better get the goods on this guy, Billy. If you need to hire a private investigator, hire the best. Get back to me one week from today."

One week later at nine A.M. in the office of Eighty-Seventh District Republican headquarters, Billy was about to make his report on Palmer.

The Boss said, "Sit down, Billy. Let's have it."

"Well," Billy said with a big smile, "I think we got him."

"Go on, go no, get to the point. Leave nothing out."

"He did fall out of the sky. One day out of the blue he showed up on the doorstep of Doc's Bar and Grill. Doc hired Palmer to be a short-order cook. Sometime later Palmer opened Palmer's Place adjacent to Doc's bar. Later he and his significant other moved into the apartment above the bar. He formed the Gibtown Business Association, ran for city council, and - ."

The Boss interrupted Billy. "I don't want to hear about Saint Palmer, I want to hear about Sinner Palmer."

"Yes, yes, I was coming to that. William Palmer is really Dr. C. William Palmer, M.D. of Philadelphia, Pennsylvania. Well, not Philadelphia but a small town just outside of Philadelphia. Dr. Palmer had quite a good practice. He also had a wife and three children, a girlfriend, a drinking problem, and a drug problem. His wife found out and divorced him. She took the house, the car, the little cottage on the lake, she got the kids, she got a huge child support and alimony, she even got the dog." The Boss let Billy continue uninterrupted. "After the divorce Palmer hit the bottle more, hit the drugs more, his girlfriend hit the road. He tried to start over and contacted an old friend from med school that had a practice in Philadelphia. It didn't work. Palmer continued down the road of drugs and booze. His friend kicked him out. He then moved into a fleabag apartment near a railroad track on the poor side of town. After more drinking and drugs, he packed up his duffel bag and left."

"Good job, Billy. Is there more?"

"Yes, I would like to tell you how we found out about Dr. C. William Palmer. It's quite a story and it did cost you some real money. You did say 'Do whatever it takes', remember? We,

rather I," Billy wanted all the credit he could get, "knew Palmer didn't fall out of the sky. So how did he just show up at Doc's Bar? Gibsonton, especially the west side of town known as Gibtown, is home to what? Carnies! They drift in and out of Gibtown all the time."

The Boss was getting interested.

"As I was saying, anyone who shows up in Gibtown out of the blue is probably a carny worker. So I went out where the carnies store their equipment during the winter and started asking if anyone knew a guy named William Palmer. One said he did. He thought that Palmer was a hobo that hooked up with Dobbs' Carnival. I checked it out and found that the owner, Dobbs, spends the winter in Ruskin. I made a trip to Ruskin to talk to Mr. Dobbs. Sure enough, Palmer worked for him. When the carnival stored their equipment for the winter, Palmer must have walked into Gibsonton and saw a help wanted sign in Doc's Bar." Billy paused, smiling with pride knowing the result his sleuthing got him.

"That's great, Billy, that's exactly what I needed."

"No, Boss. There's more. The details are very important to the end results."

"Ok, Billy."

"While visiting Dobbs I found that Dr. C. William Palmer died while traveling with the Dobbs Carnival! They buried him in the pauper section of the Hillsborough Cemetery. The funeral service of Dr. C. William Palmer was at the Smalley Funeral Home of Gibsonton. But, and here's where things get even better: Dr. Palmer had a traveling companion named Andy Miller. Miller also worked for Dobbs' Carnival and took all of

Dr. Palmer's personal effects with him when the carnival stored their equipment..."

Van Buren hit the punch line, "And Miller assumed Palmer's identity! Oh, that is good!" Van Buren was smiling now too, his mind racing with all kinds of stories Miller, if he was indeed Miller, might be hiding.

Billy went on with his story, "We don't know too much about this Andy Miller guy. We do know whatever his past is he doesn't want anyone to know about it, whatever the circumstances are, good or bad.

The Boss sat back with a puff of smoke from his cigar. Billy was right. It was worth hearing all the details of this story. "Excellent work, Billy!" Billy couldn't have been happier if he'd won the lottery.

Van Buren continued, "I think you're right that our new Dr. Palmer is likely Andy Miller, and we're going to call his bluff. I believe that Andy Miller is going to stay Dr. C. William Palmer forever. Miller must have more to hide than Dr. C. William Palmer if he's willing to assume an identity filled with failure, adultery, drugs, booze, hobos, and carny workers. For all we know, Miller might have killed someone somewhere. To that end is the story of Dr. C. William Palmer."

Chapter 30

The Boss congratulated Billy once more, then picked up the phone and buzzed his secretary.

"Yes, Boss?"

"Get William Palmer on the phone for me. He will probably be at his restaurant."

Moments later The Boss's phone rang. "Yes."

His secretary said, "I have Mr. Palmer on the line."

He thanked his secretary and was connected to Skeeter. "Mr. Palmer, this is Jerome Van Buren. I would like to come to your restaurant and have a talk with you. Could we meet tomorrow at ten A.M.?"

Skeeter said, "That sounds good, ten a.m. tomorrow."

"See you then."

Skeeter slowly hung up the phone wondering why the head of the Republican Party would be calling him. *I'm a*

nobody. Why does he want a personal meeting with me? Does he meet with all opposing candidates? Why me? Am I letting my paranoia get the best of me? Or does he know something about the killings back in Durand? Does he know about me taking Palmer's identity? Does he know about all the lying, lying, lying I've done in the past?

The next morning at ten A.M. sharp, The Boss, Billy, and The Boss's bodyguard, Chuck Buzzer, entered Palmer's Place. Chuck the bodyguard, is a big man, he is six foot four and weighs two hundred forty pounds, broad at the shoulder and narrow at the hip. He doesn't say much. He doesn't have to. When things get tense, The Boss says "I would like to meet my friend Chuck."

Gail was working as hostess and recognized the huge Van Buren and his entourage when he entered the restaurant. Skeeter had informed her that he would be meeting with Mr. Van Buren, the Chairman of the Republican Party today. As he entered the restaurant he took his hat off and announced, "My name is Jerome Van Buren," he said while scanning the room. "I have an appointment with Mr. Palmer."

Gail knew who he was. Everyone did. "Right this way, please. I will let Mr. Palmer know you are here." Gail had never called Palmer, "Mr. Palmer" before."

Skeeter, with a smile on his face and an outstretched hand, came to the table where The Boss was sitting with his hands perched on his cane standing in front of him. "Glad to finally meet you, Mr. Van Buren."

The Boss shook Skeeter's hand and said, "This is my associate, William Lee, and my friend Chuck Buzzer," referring to them both.

Skeeter sat down still smiling and said, "What can I do for you gentlemen?"

The Boss said, "I will get right to the point, Mr. Palmer…" Van Buren said with emphasis on his name. He paused and looked straight into Skeeter's eyes, "but we both know that's not your real name, now is it? We always like to know all about our competition." Continuing to look at Skeeter, he held out his hand toward Billy. Billy knew what The Boss wanted. With a look like a cat that ate the canary, Billy opened a folder he was carrying and pulled out a piece of paper, and gave it to The Boss. He took it and never stopped looking at Skeeter. "It says here that Dr. C. William Palmer, M.D. of Gibsonton, Florida is actually Dr. C. William Palmer, M.D. who happens to have had a failed medical practice, wife, three children, a girlfriend, a drinking and drug problem, became a hobo and carny worker,..." another pause for effect, "and died." Dr. Palmer, or should I say, Andy Miller, would that be correct?"

Skeeter turned white and started to sweat. His heart was beating fast. He knew the jig was up. He just couldn't *lie, lie, lie* his way out of this. He dropped his head then looked up straight into Van Buren's face. He was going to continue with one lie. He was going to be Andy Miller, not Skeeter Jones the murderer. Skeeter was almost out of breath. "Yes, it's true."

"Mr. Miller, I don't want to ruin you."

"What do you want to do?"

"I believe there is a way out for both of us. I would like to see you drop out of the State House of Representative race. Use any reason. Continue with your restaurant business and president of the Gibtown Business Association. Run for Gibsonton City Council again. Someday run for State Representative again. Maybe more. Of course, I would like you to run as a Republican. I would be there for you, helping and advising you. Or…"

"Or you will ruin me."

The Boss, in what appeared to be a genuine manner, said, "This is a big decision. Let me know what you think. Not today, not tomorrow, sometime soon, let's say two or three days from now. Say by Friday at ten o'clock. Here is my card, Mr. Palmer. Give me a call. By Friday at ten o'clock."

The Boss and his entourage left the restaurant. Skeeter just sat there dumbfounded. A few minutes later, Beverly came over to Skeeter's table. She took one look at him and said, "What's wrong with you? Looks like you saw a ghost."

Skeeter could not believe this was happening. He realized he would always be under the control of Jerome Van Buren. If they could trace him back to Andy Miller, chances are they could go farther, to his real identity as Skeeter Jones, murderer. Beverly was at Skeeter's side, when she touched his shoulder he finally responded, "Oh. Nothing, nothing at all. I just need some fresh air. I think I'm going to go for a walk."

Chapter 31

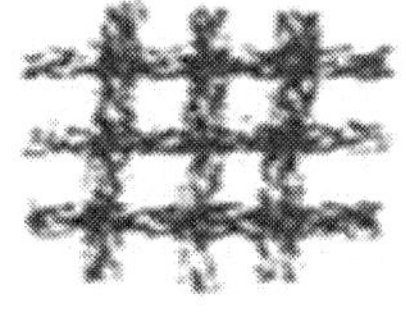

Skeeter got up from the table, left the restaurant, and walked around Gibtown for about an hour. He returned to the restaurant where his car was, got in, and drove to the Chase Bank in Gibsonton. It was now eleven-thirty A.M.

Once at the bank Skeeter transferred fifty thousand dollars from the Palmer's Place restaurant account that he and Doc shared to a new account. He established an ATM card with a password. He purchased a cashier's check for twenty thousand and withdrew five thousand in cash. While at the bank, the teller who knew Skeeter quite well from previous visits at the bank, said, "Are you alright, Mr. Palmer? You look a little under the weather."

"No, I'm just fine. Just a little tired, that's all."

Skeeter left the bank, got back into his car, and drove to the restaurant. He did not go into the restaurant but went up to his and Beverly's apartment. Everything seemed so surreal.

He immediately went to his desk and sat down. Opening a drawer he pulled out three business-sized white envelopes. On one envelope he wrote *Beverly* and placed the twenty thousand dollar cashier's check inside. On another, he wrote *Doc*. On the third envelope, he wrote *Mary Lou Jones* and addressed it to the house that he and Mary Lou shared in Byron, Michigan. He placed the account number worth fifty-thousand dollars and the ATM card inside. He proceeded to write three letters. The first, to Mary Lou.

With tears in his eyes he started:

Dear Mary,
I have not stopped thinking of you and the kids. I wanted to call and talk with you and send money. I was afraid the police would find out where I was and I would be put in jail or worse, killed by the mob. I deposited fifty-thousand dollars in a savings account with Chase Bank. I have enclosed an ATM card and the account number. Use them to help with your and the kids' expenses. Do not use the same ATM twice in a row. There are Chase Banks in Flint and Lansing, I believe there is a branch in Byron now. I will not be able to make contact with you again.

With Love,
Skeeter

The second letter was to Beverly. He explained the best he could about what happened with Jerome Van Buren. That he had been married, had children, and was a doctor. Of course, that was a lie, he was Skeeter Jones, murderer of three people back in Michigan. He had to maintain the C. William Palmer identity. So he did what he did best. He *lied, lied, lied.* It was the best for all. Along with the twenty-thousand dollar cashier's check, Skeeter signed the title to his brand new car to Beverly.

Dear Beverly,
I have asked Doc to let you stay in the apartment for as long as you want. I will never be able to make contact with you again. I will miss you terribly.

Love,
Palmer

The third letter was to Doc. He again lied in his explanation of what happened. He told Doc that he had withdrawn seventy-five thousand dollars from their mutual bank account. That he gave twenty thousand to Beverly, sent fifty-thousand to his wife and children, and kept five thousand for himself. The lie wasn't that he gave fifty-thousand to his wife and kids, it was to which wife. Doc would believe it was to C. William Palmer's wife and kids in Pennsylvania.

Keeping track of lies becomes more difficult each time we tell them. What a web we weave.

Skeeter also signed over his Palmer's Place restaurant ownership to Doc and all remaining money in their mutual bank account. Skeeter told Doc that he was more than a friend and partner; he was more like a father than his real father had been.

It was twelve-thirty P.M. Skeeter sealed the three envelopes. He placed Beverly's and Doc's on the kitchen table. Mary Lou's envelope he stamped and placed in his coat pocket to be mailed from a different town, maybe a different state so that it could not be traced back to Gibsonton.

Skeeter then went to the bedroom. He opened the closet door and on the top shelf retrieved his old duffel bag. After a short inventory, he closed the bag. He dressed in an old pair of overalls, a heavy plaid shirt, old leather boots and topped it all off with his fedora hat with a hole in the front. Except for the hat, he was dressed the same way he was when he committed the murders back in Durand.

He picked up his duffel bag and flung it over his shoulder. Without a backward glance, he left the apartment, got into his car, and drove to the Bethany Flower Shop in Gibtown. He purchased a lovely flowering plant.

Leaving the shop he drove forty-five miles to the cemetery where the real Dr. C. William Palmer was buried. He pulled into the cemetery, a little disoriented as to the location of his friend's grave. He drove to the back where the indigent lay in peace.

It was difficult to find Palmer's gravesite. This part of the cemetery was not well maintained. Most of the graves had no

markers at all, some were marked with a simple wooden marker that had fallen over or rotted away. Skeeter kept looking.

He knew that Palmer's grave was at the very back of the cemetery close to the railroad tracks. He often thought what a great location that was for Palmer; he could hear the trains as they went by.

Finally, he found it. Skeeter looked down at the bronze marker that Martha Smalley picked out for him. Dr. C. William Palmer, M.D., his date of birth and date of death.

Skeeter wondered *Who has been taking care of Palmer's grave?* It was apparent that someone had been tending the gravesite. The grass was cut away, the marker clean, and a withered bouquet of flowers was placed on the marker. Of course, Martha Smalley. It had to be her. Skeeter was right. Martha Smalley of Smalley's Funeral Home came to Palmer's grave, cut the grass with small hand clippers, watered, and placed flowers on his grave.

There seemed to be from the start a real feeling between Skeeter and Martha, a sort of a mother-son relationship. Skeeter did not know Martha Smalley had passed away two months ago. Leonard sold his funeral home to Roy, his former employee. Leonard still lived in the apartment over the funeral home and assisted Roy with funerals from time to time.

Skeeter stayed for an hour or so looking at the bronze marker and looking at the railroad tracks about one hundred feet away. He left the cemetery and started driving back to Gibsonton.

He arrived at his restaurant in Gibsonton and parked his car in the garage. He got out of his car, reached back inside and retrieved his duffel bag, and put on his fedora.

Leaving the garage he looked around making sure no one was in sight. He walked the short distance to the road. He was sure no one would recognize him dressed as a hobo. He headed east in the direction of the storage area of Dobbs' Carnival.

He walked a mile or so until he came to a single set of railroad tracks, the same one that he crossed the first day he entered Gibsonton. On the side of the road next to the tracks was the same sign that read Gibsonton Poultry Farm. He walked to the center of the tracks. He looked one way then the other and said, "Which way should we go Palmer?" and started walking.

As he walked on he started to reflect on his past: Born in the small town of Byron, Michigan, Huckleberry Finn childhood, a job at the chicken farm, three years in the Army, worked on the railroad as a gandy dancer for Grand Trunk Railroad, married Mary Lou and had a houseful of kids, and oh, yes, let's not forget the three people he killed at the 602 Bar, rode the rails with Palmer, worked for Dobb's Carnival, met Beverly and Doc, and got into politics. To think that a person such as himself could go to a town like Gibtown in Gibsonton and become an important part of the community.

Feeling sad to leave Doc, Beverly, and Gibtown, at the same time wondering what the future holds. Suddenly Skeeter realized *What future*? He could never go back to Byron and Mary Lou, he couldn't go back to Doc and Beverly and the life he had in Gibtown. There would always be a Jerome Van Buren

that would uncover his past. Skeeter believed that back in Michigan the police had probably given up on finding him. The case had grown cold. The mob would never give up. They would wait, and wait, and wait. One day somewhere they would be there for him.

Skeeter continued in his thoughts. *Maybe I will meet another Palmer. Maybe I will mentor a new lost soul. Maybe. Just keep walking, Skeeter, just keep walking.*

Some day when you stop at a railroad crossing waiting for the train to go by and you see a thin man wearing an old fedora with a hole in the front flashing a big smile, that just might be my friend Skeeter Jones. Smile back and say hello for me.

The End

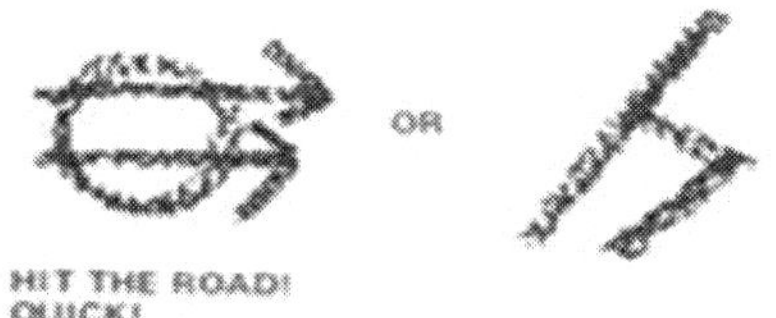

Acknowledgments

In the old days when a writer would submit a book to be printed, they would submit a manuscript, a hard copy of the book. Not so today, you have to do everything electronically. You have to send the front and back covers and the spine separately and you have to make sure the left and right margins are set in specific dimensions. There is a lot to it. Guess what. I have almost as much computer and electronic talent as I do for spelling, grammar, and the fine arts, which is zero. But I do know someone who has those skills. He is a very nice looking man, he looks like his father, that would be me. Actually, he is nice looking, unlike his father. His name is Cary Vaughn. He is very talented in the use of computers as well as being a CPA.

Let's not forget the importance of first reads. When you think you finally have the book complete - it's been written and edited, illustrated, all the technical, and computer work is done, the font and line spacing chosen - you think you're ready to go, right? NO! One more thing. You should have two or three people read the book who were not part of putting the book together. First readers. They read the book simply as a reader. Are you telling a story, does it actually have a beginning, middle, and end, and is it interesting? They will be the real test of the book's readability and possibly its worth.

So I thank you, my first readers, Ron and Gail Sipes, Quentin Brainerd, and Elizabeth Wehman who is the co-founder and president of the Shiawassee Area Writers. She also has books on Amazon.

If you like the book, *Skeeter Jones.* I thank you. If you like the way the book reads and the illustrations, Sherri deserves

credit. If you like the layout of the book, Cary deserves the credit. Gee, I wonder what I did.

Thanks for reading my book!

A Note About the Writing

My first book, *BUTCH* was a memoir which is simply a book based on the author's personal memories. Whatever the author recalls, that's what it is.

Memoirs need editing, for sure. But not like a novel. In my opinion, a novel is a horse of a different color. Many novels are fiction. That means the writer has to make up the entire story. They have to create the setting, tone, and characters with feelings and convey those emotions through the use of actions and dialogue, to keep the reader interested, and finally bring it all to a conclusion. The writer has to describe, describe, ***describe*** (I'm pretty sure my editor was tired of saying it and I was tired of hearing it). The author needs to invite the reader to observe what is happening through words. This is where the editor comes in. At least this is where mine came in.

The process of creating all the parts necessary to make a work of fiction required much more effort than recalling my memories. Although I could see my characters in my mind - I could imagine what they felt or did - that made sense to me, I needed to write so my reader could also see and hear the characters the way I did. This was not easy. There were many times I would say, "Doesn't it make sense the character would be feeling this way? Why do I have to describe it?" or "The character would be shouting in this scene" but then there was nothing to let the reader know how the character was speaking.

During the initial read-throughs (and there were many) my editor asked me what gestures the characters were making - did the person slam his hand down when making a point or

throw his hands in the air? What were they thinking or feeling - did the woman fall to her knees when receiving the news or silently cry? How were they talking - were they whispering or shouting? What was the scene around them - was it at a crowded bar or along a wooded path?

Creating the plot was not all that difficult, but there were times when through the editing process, we found that a minor tweak was needed in one place but created a timeline problem in another. This would result in making major changes to what a character did or when they did it, and then we needed to see if our changes affected other parts of the book. This process at times became quite daunting.

Unlike my memoir *BUTCH*, *Skeeter Jones* contained dialogue, which requires punctuation. Lots of punctuation. Let's just say punctuation is not my forte, and leave it at that.

I spent countless hours on the phone with my editor while we both stared at our screens in Google Docs seeing the changes happening on both our screens.

Other times my editor would make changes on her own, in a different color, cross things out, or make comments on the side to come back to later when we could both be online at the same time and talk through the possible changes.

Bringing this novel to completion was definitely a learning process; one that I'm sure will be beneficial for my next book, as soon as my editor recovers.

SKEETER JONES______________________________

Made in the USA
Columbia, SC
04 July 2022

62778643R00126